SHERLOCK SHOLMES

vs.

FANTÔMAS

SHERLOCK HOLMES

vs.

FANTÔMAS

(Bandits in Black Coats)

A drama in 5 acts by
Pierre de Wattyne & Yorril Walter

translated and adapted by
Frank J. Morlock

A Black Coat Press Book

To my beloved Gaby.
FJM

Visit our website at www.blackcoatpress.com

ISBN 978-1-934543-67-2. First Printing. February 2009. Published by Black Coat Press, an imprint of Hollywood Comics.com, LLC, P.O. Box 17270, Encino, CA 91416. All rights reserved.

Introduction

The stage play translated here as *Sherlock Holmes vs. Fantômas* was originally entitled *La Mort de Herlock Sholmès, ou Bandits en habit noir*, i.e.: "The Death of Herlock Sholmes, or Bandits in Black Coats," a name which, as we shall discuss, raises some tantalizing fictional possibilities.

The play opened in Brussels in the early summer of 1914 and closed when the Great War broke out in July, which effectively put an end to its stage life. It has never been performed since. It was registered with the Belgian Editorial Office in Brussels, as is the custom; a copy was located by Frank J. Morlock at John Hopkins University. But curiously, the play is not in their catalogue. To say that it has been mostly forgotten today is no understatement.

Its authors are almost as obscure. Pierre de Wattyne is the *nom-de-plume* of Belgian writer and playwright Pierre Van de Wattyne. De Wattyne appears to have penned, alone or in collaboration, numerous plays, vaudevilles, melodramas, etc. between 1910 and 1950. He and another Belgian playwright, Yorril Hanswyck (whose last name also appears in various records as Hansewick and Haneswick), collaborated on a number of *Grand-Guignol* plays, including the famous *L'Expérience du Docteur* Lorde [*Dr. Lorde's Experiment*] (adapted from Cyril-Berger) in 1922. The list of de Wattyne's works include *Le Vieux* [*The Old Man*] and *Oh! La Vache* [*Oh! The Cow*], two 1912 vaudevilles, also written in collaboration with the same Yorril Walter who co-signed *Bandits en habit noir, Le Sorcier*

Rouge [*The Red Wizard*], a 5-act drama adapted from Fabrice Delphi's novel, and, later, a collection of folk tales from his native Flanders, *Les Bonnes Flandres*, and two murder mysteries: *Les deux assassins* [*The Two Murderers*] and *Les doigts truqués* [*The Trick Fingers*] in 1943. Novels of note include *Le crucifié de Grenade* [*The Crucified Man of Granada*], *Le bar des colorés* [*The Coloreds' Bar*] and *L'Immense amour de Soledad* [*Soledad's Great Love*]. As for Yorril Walter, there is no information readily available about him.

Bandits en habit noir was not the first unauthorized Sherlock Holmes pastiche. As had been the case with the character of Lord Ruthven almost a century before, which had given rise to a number of French "sequels",[1] the popularity of Sherlock Holmes fostered its own pantheon of contemporary imitations.

The first writer to tackle the burgeoning myth was Maurice Leblanc, who decided to pit his hero, the gentleman-burglar Arsène Lupin, against Sherlock Holmes in the short story *Sherlock Holmes arrive trop tard*, [*Sherlock Holmes Arrives Too Late*], published in *Je Sais Tout* No. 17 in June 1906.[2] Later, Leblanc changed the name to "Herlock Sholmès," but went on to tell more stories about the two arch-rivals in *Arsène Lupin contre Herlock Sholmès* (1907)[3] and *L'Aiguille Creuse* [*The Hollow Needle*] (1909). The popularity of the concept

---

[1] See the Black Coat Press editions *Lord Ruthven the Vampire* (ISBN 1932983104) and *The Return of Lord Ruthven* (ISBN 1932983112).

[2] Included in the Black Coat Press edition of *Arsène Lupin vs. Sherlock Holmes: The Hollow Needle* (ISBN 0974971196).

[3] Published by Black Coat Press as *Arsène Lupin vs. Sherlock Holmes: The Blonde Phantom* (ISBN 1932983147).

even led Leblanc to license an original stage play, written by Victor Darlay and Henry de Gorsse, performed in Paris in 1910.[4]

Meanwhile, in Germany, the series of pulp magazines which eventually led to the creation of the character known today as "Harry Dickson" had begun in January 1907 under the title of *Detectiv Sherlock Holmes und Seine Weltberühmten Abenteuer* [*Sherlock Holmes and His Most Famous Cases*]. Published by Verlagshaus für Volksliteratur und Kunst, the series comprised 230 issues in total and ended in June 1911. The name Sherlock Holmes was used in the first ten issues, then changed to *Aus dem Geheimakten des Weltdetektivs* [*The Secret Files of the King of Detectives*]. Eventually, in later incarnations, that detective came to be called Harry Dickson (his original Doctor Watson, had been named Harry Taxson), and inherited a younger sidekick named Tom Wills.[5]

Then, there was the detective "Herlokholms," who appeared alongside Allan Dickson, the star of *Allan Dickson, the King of Australian Detectives*, a short-lived but popular French pulp series initially created in 1909 by Arnould Galopin under the pseudonym of "Max Dearly." In *L'Homme au Complet Gris* [*The Man in the Grey Suit* a.k.a. *The Man in Grey*] (1912),[6] a young

---

[4] Published by Black Coat Press as *Arsène Lupin vs. Sherlock Holmes: The Stage Play* (ISBN 1932983163).

[5] A first volume of Harry Dickson's adventures, *The Heir of Dracula*, is scheduled to be published by Black Coat Press.

[6] Arnould Galopin is the author of *Doctor Omega*, published by Black Coat Press (ISBNs 0974071102 and 09740781110). *The Man in the Grey* is scheduled to be published by Black Coat Press.

Dickson and Holmes team up to solve the mystery of Jack the Ripper. For the record, Galopin had already used a detective named "Cherlokolls" the year before in his serial *Le tour du monde en aéroplane* [*Around the World in an Airplane*] written with Henri de la Vaulx.

Even the rather Oedipal concept of murdering Holmes to make room for a newer, younger detective was created in *L'Assassinat du plus célèbre détective* [*The Murder of the Most Famous of Detectives*], the very first issue of the *Miss Boston* series by Antonin Reschal, published in 1911, in which the plucky female detective began her career by investigating the murder of her more famous predecessor.

It is in this literary context that *Bandits en habit noir* was written and presented to the public. It was no coincidence that the *Habits Noirs*, the Black Coats, was the title of a still-popular series of novels by Paul Féval, featuring the eponymous criminal conspiracy.[7] In 1908, episode 6 of Victorin Jasset's popular French film serial *Nick Carter, le Roi des Détectives* had, in fact, also been entitled *Les Bandits en habit noir*, proving the continuing allure of the concept.

In order to not spoil the reader's enjoyment, we will address other issues concerning Sherlock Holmes, Fantômas and Harry Dickson in the Afterword.

Jean-Marc Lofficier

---

[7] Four volumes of that series have, so far, been published by Black Coat Press: *'Salem Street* (ISBN 9781932983463), *The Invisible Weapon* (ISBN 9781932983807), *The Parisian Jungle* (ISBN 9781934543030), *The Companions of the Treasure* (ISBN 9781934543269), with the other three to follow.

SHERLOCK HOLMES

vs.

FANTÔMAS

Characters

Sherlock Holmes
Fantômas (a.k.a. Doctor Garrick, Tom Bob, Sâr Ha-mashkim, etc.)

in order of appearance:
Emily Holmes, Holmes' niece
Antonia Gruff, Emily's servant
Harry Dickson, a young aspiring detective
Roger Walter, Emily's fiancé
Inspector Lestrade, of Scotland Yard
Vachard, Fantômas' lieutenant and a member of the
Black Coats criminal brotherhood
A clerk, various policemen, workers, bandits, etc.

The action takes place in London in late 1906 or
early 1907.

ACT I

At Sherlock Holmes' Baker Street residence.

The stage represents a room. In the back, there is another room. There are two doors, left and right. There is a desk to the left of the audience and a table at the right.

AT RISE, Mrs. Gruff is sorting out some papers on the desk. Emily enters.

EMILY: (*in the doorway*) What are you doing, Mrs. Gruff?

MRS. GRUFF: As you can see, Miss Emily, I'm putting a little order in all these scribblings.

EMILY: Please, don't! You know that my uncle forbids us to touch or move anything, no matter how trivial.

MRS. GRUFF: But look at the mess!

EMILY: You're going to get us into trouble. That's all we need.

MRS. GRUFF: It's more than I can bear! I have to straighten up, to arrange things. I've always been an orderly woman and at my age, you don't change.

EMILY: Would you prefer Mr. Holmes to be angry all night?

MRS. GRUFF: My God! As if that would make a differ-
ence! If he doesn't sulk for one reason, it's
for another. He's always in a bad mood.

EMILY: All the more reason not to exasperate him.

MRS. GRUFF: I understand, Miss Emily. I won't touch
anything anymore. But it's really difficult for
me. If I do my job properly, cleaning up and
straightening up things, I get yelled at, but if
I don't do anything, you're going to say,
poor old Mrs. Gruff doesn't know how to
keep a house in order.

EMILY: I would never say such a thing!

MRS. GRUFF: But if... if... Ah! That will teach me to
try to help some people!

EMILY: Now, now, Mrs. Gruff, forget what I said.

MRS. GRUFF: I'm the widow of a constable, Miss Emily. I have a pension that allows me to live
without being in service. My daughter Margot must have told you this...

EMILY: No, I don't recall that she spoke of you.

MRS. GRUFF: That doesn't surprise me. My Margot
isn't much of a talker. But she likes you very
much. When she speaks of her master, she
speaks fulsomely. Mr. Holmes this, Miss
Emily that. You have a fine servant in her.

She really does like you.

EMILY: Why, it's mutual. We like her, as well.

MRS. GRUFF: That's good! When she came to visit me, the other night, and she fell ill all of a sudden, the Doctor said, "My poor girl, you're very weak, you absolutely must have country air and a complete rest." She almost didn't hear him because she was struggling to leave. "It's impossible," she said, "I can't abandon Mr. Holmes like that. I must continue my service until he's found someone to replace me." So I said, "Don't be difficult, child, your old mother will take up your apron, so that your master won't be in a fix, and you will find your place still waiting when you're ready to return." Could have I done any better?

EMILY: Surely not.

MRS. GRUFF: So I sent Margot straight to Scotland, to stay with my brother, Henry, to rest.

EMILY: But why didn't she come to see us and say good-bye before she left?

MRS. GRUFF: Feeble as she was, I didn't think it would have been wise for the poor dear to travel back to your place. Besides, since I had to replace her all the same, I thought you could learn the story from my mouth as easily as from hers.

EMILY: I was quite astonished to see you, as I was unaware of your existence.

MRS. GRUFF: But I showed you my papers, all in order
they were. Mr. Holmes examined them, and
he knows all about papers.

EMILY: (*smiling*) Yes, he does.

(*Harry Dickson enters. He is a young man of not yet 20,
with a strong, virile face.*)

DICKSON: Excuse me, am I disturbing you?

EMILY: Come in, Mr. Dickson. I hope you haven't forgotten your promise.

DICKSON: What promise?

EMILY: To watch your language.

DICKSON: Don't worry, I'll be careful.

EMILY: Mrs. Gruff, offer a seat to Mr. Dickson.

DICKSON: Don't disturb the old bat, I'll get it myself.

EMILY: Mr. Dickson, you're already forgetting our
agreement.

DICKSON: Excuse me, Miss Emily, I'm just an uncouth
American.

MRS. GRUFF: No need to say it, it's plain for all to see.

DICKSON: Just like your false hair and false teeth, old woman.

EMILY: Sir!

DICKSON: Excuse me, Miss Emily. In the future, I'll try to be more civilized.

EMILY: Good!

DICKSON: I'll behave... Has the old codger, I mean, Mr. Holmes, returned yet?

EMILY: Mr. Dickson, you are incorrigible! A whiskey?

DICKSON: With soda. All right!

EMILY: I'm trying to be nice to you. You're a tenant in this house, too, and I believe in good relations with the neighbors.

DICKSON: You're spoiling me, Miss Emily. You're spoiling me so much that the notion of living without you has become unthinkable.

EMILY: Why, Mr. Dickson, is that a compliment?

DICKSON: And still, you plan to marry that no-good Roger Walter!

EMILY: Quiet, you bad boy! Now, that's a ridiculous supposition.

DICKSON: Why? Am I mistaken?

EMILY: Absolutely!

DICKSON: So your heart is still free? The place is still
           to let?

EMILY: Still.

DICKSON: Then it's a deal. I'll take it.

EMILY: What are you talking about?

DICKSON: As much room as I can get.

EMILY: You're not serious, Mr. Dickson.

DICKSON: I am! You're the one who isn't serious. You
           have before you your most ardent suitor, and
           yet the one you listen to least.

EMILY: Self-pity doesn't become you, Mr. Dickson.
          You are the only man I've allowed to pay me
          court. That's sufficiently compromising.

DICKSON: Ah, if I wasn't still a student...

EMILY: South Kensington is a very respectable univer-
          sity.

DICKSON: But I'm not earning the kind of living that
           would enable me to support a wife...

EMILY: Do be quiet! Smoke your pipe. It will keep you patient while waiting for my uncle who ought to return any minute now. You can then play your game of backgammon.

DICKSON: Mr. Holmes has been coming home very late these days. We barely have time for more than one game.

EMILY: Don't complain too much. You make up for it by having drinks with your friend Mr. Vernon.

DICKSON: Not at all. I haven't seen James in days.

EMILY: What? Your inseparable friend has disappeared?

DICKSON: Yes, rather abruptly, too. He cast me off like an old shoe. It's my fault though.

EMILY: How so?

DICKSON: I told him that I always have about my person a famous Indian poison which I got from Mr. Triggs... (*pulling out a small flask*) He was so frightened that I haven't seen him since. What a coward! I really miss him, though, because we were good friends.

EMILY: But you hadn't known him for very long.

DICKSON: Only two weeks. But he knew my cousin Freddy, so we were like old comrades.

EMILY: Was it your cousin who introduced him to you?

DICKSON: No. My cousin's in New York. It was James himself who accosted me, saying, "Hello, are you Harry Dickson, the junior boxing champion of Queens, the cousin of Frederick Dickson, one of the rising stars of the New York police force? If so, I'm a friend of your cousin. My name's James Vernon, and I would love to shake your hand and become your friend, too." I said, "Shake!" and from that moment, we were best friends. Besides, he played a mean game of backgammon, like me. He liked boxing, and whiskey, like me. And he insisted on always paying for the drinks.

EMILY: Like you?

DICKSON: No. That was the sole point on which we had different ideas. But it didn't damage our friendship, quite the contrary.

EMILY: You are a bit of a miser, aren't you, Mr. Dickson? I know for a fact that you carry a good bit of money on you.

DICKSON: Be quiet about that! It wouldn't do for the London pickpockets to learn that I always carry all my savings on me.

EMILY: Why not hide them in your flat?

DICKSON: Because my savings are better defended by my fists than in a room with useless bolts.

EMILY: So, in short, your friend Mr. Vernon doesn't come to see you any more, doesn't pay for your drinks, and no longer plays backgammon with you?

DICKSON: Alas! I'm as sad as an old Scottish ballad. But let's speak of something else. Your uncle shouldn't wander the streets so late at night. The neighborhood isn't very safe. There are a lot of dubious types about and, well, you know...

EMILY: Continue your thought, Mr. Dickson.

DICKSON: You know what I mean.

EMILY: No, I don't. You have some concernd, I see. Pray tell me, what is it all about?

DICKSON: Well, I prefer to speak to you because your uncle has a difficult character. All the same, I have the greatest respect for him, because he doesn't suffer from cold feet. Well, he's taken it into his head to arrest Fantômas, that mysterious criminal whom everyone suspects, but no one knows a thing about. He's never spoken to you about it?

EMILY: Never. You know he never mentions his investigations to me.

DICKSON: What about Mr. Walter?

EMILY: Even less. When Roger became his private secretary, he swore never to divulge a professional secret. And he knows how to keep his word.

DICKSON: Even with you?

EMILY: Especially with me. He knows that I think the more of him for it.

DICKSON: By God! It isn't worth being the niece of the king of detectives if you've never heard of Fantômas.

EMILY: The newspapers assure us that Fantômas doesn't exist. He is just the invention of some French journalists.

DICKSON: Scotland Yard denies his existence because they're unable to catch him.

EMILY: But what crimes do they charge him with?

DICKSON: All those that have remained unsolved for the past seven years. Fantômas terrorizes the city. He reigns through mystery and fear. One day, you find a note signed Fantômas on your table, in your desk drawer, under your pillow. Then you ask yourself how the note got there. You waste your time questioning the staff, but you'll never find out. Still, Fantômas' terms are clear: he commands you to deposit a portion of your fortune secretly in a place indicated by him, or to destroy important papers, or more; he imposes other sacrifices on you that you must perform immediately.

EMILY: And if the person refuses to do it?

DICKSON: It's quite simple. Anyone who dares disobey Fantômas' orders is found drowned in his bath, charred inside his flaming house, or stabbed to death in his bed.

MRS. GRUFF: He is said to appear in the most terrifying and diverse attires.

EMILY: And it's this formidable monster that my uncle intends to arrest?

DICKSON: And he'll do it before long.

MRS. GRUFF: Has Mr. Holmes confided in you?

DICKSON: No, that's not in his nature. But I've observed a little gleam in his eye that speaks volumes. Even when he loses at backgammon, and loses almost three pounds, which is enormous, he has a way of saying, "It's fine, it's fine," which augurs no good for Fantômas.

MRS. GRUFF: If those are the only clues you have…

DICKSON: Believe me, they're enough.

MRS. GRUFF: You're very confident.

DICKSON: And you, very incredulous. One would almost believe you didn't want this wretch to be caught.

MRS. GRUFF: Me? May God preserve me! A bandit who even kidnaps women to extort money.

DICKSON: If he carried you off, it would be a joke. The luggage would remain uncollected in the cloak room.

(*The door bell rings.*)

EMILY: Please answer that, Mrs. Gruff. Who can it be, at this hour?

(*Exit Mrs. Gruff.*)

DICKSON: Perhaps your uncle forgot his key?

EMILY: Him? Never. But if I'm not mistaken, it's Mr. Walter.

(*Roger Walter enters, followed by Mrs. Gruff. Roger is dressed in formal dinner wear.*)

ROGER: Good evening, Miss Emily. Evening, Dickson. The Master isn't here?

EMILY: No, he hasn't returned yet.

ROGER: At this hour?... It's getting late.

EMILY: That's what we were saying. We were worried about Fantômas.

ROGER: Hush! Don't mention that name aloud.

EMILY: It seems you've known about this for a while?

ROGER: Did Dickson tell you that?

DICKSON: And may I add that, if you, Mr. Walter, or your employer, ever find this bandit's hideout, don't go to Scotland Yard. They don't know how to do things properly. Come to me, Harry Dickson, former boxing champion, and I'll take care of it.

EMILY: (*to Roger*) I wasn't expecting you this evening. And in formal attire?

ROGER: I have a mission to fulfill. But first, I need instructions from the Master.

DICKSON: Say, Mrs. Gruff, when are you going to serve supper?

MRS. GRUFF: What?

DICKSON: Miss Emily agrees with me, don't you, Emily?

EMILY: Well, I...

MRS. GRUFF: I'll go, I'll go. Everybody orders me around here, even strangers.

DICKSON: Don't fret. Be kind to young lovers. Your turn will come.

(*Exit Mrs. Gruff.*)

EMILY: Really, Mr. Dickson, you're not nice to poor Mrs. Gruff. She did us a great service by coming here to replace her daughter.

DICKSON: I can't help it. I can't stand that woman.

ROGER: She's not at all like her daughter.

DICKSON: Oh, no, I had a cap for Margot.

EMILY: A cap?

DICKSON: Not one you put on your head. A crush, what.

EMILY: For her, too?

ROGER: What do you mean, "for her, too?"

EMILY: Don't you know? Mr. Dickson declared his love for me just now.

ROGER: Ah, the wretch!

DICKSON: Come on, I was just wasting my breath with Miss Emily, but with Margot, things were going fine. I used to accompany her to the butcher, the baker…

EMILY: You got the best pickings together.

DICKSON: Right. I even went with her to a seer not long ago.

ROGER: A seer? What did he say?

DICKSON: I waited at the door. She didn't want to tell me.

EMILY: (*sarcastic*) Secrets before marriage. An ill omen.

ROGER: Dickson, if Mrs. Gruff knew that her daughter was seeing you in this way…

EMILY: …She'd force you to marry her at once.

DICKSON: Now I know why I can't stand the old bird. She's my future mother-in-law. And on that note, I'll skedaddle.

EMILY: Make sure you don't hurt yourself.

DICKSON: (*laughing*) Nah. It's just something we say in New York. It means I'm going. Have a good evening, and tell Master Holmes that he's a fool to wander the streets so late at night and make me miss my game of back-gammon. Good night!

(*Dickson leaves.*)

ROGER: It's pretty, that cushion you're embroidering.

EMILY: Do you like it?

ROGER: With threads of gold, blue and green, what is there not to like. (*pause*) It doesn't bother you to work in such a poor light?

EMILY: Not at all.

ROGER: Still, the colors change. But you must know their palette by heart?

EMILY: Yes, of course.

ROGER: How your fingers come and go, intertwine, work without ever resting. Fairy fingers. I would like to kiss them.

EMILY: Please…

ROGER: Do you love me?

EMILY: Yes.

ROGER: A lot?

EMILY: A lot. What about you?

ROGER: What a question! Why else did I become your uncle's secretary – a man who is mostly grumpy, and often forgets to pay my wages?

Because I you, Emily. Do I have to repeat that to you every day?

EMILY: Yes.

ROGER: I do intend to. Once a meek engineering student, I became an amateur detective, I, who detest adventures, and all for the love of you and to earn the good will of the great Sherlock Holmes, who keeps all admirers at bay and doesn't want his niece to marry. Is it true?

EMILY: Yes, but...

ROGER: No more "buts."

EMILY: Yet, this has been going on for six months, and we are no further ahead than the first day.

ROGER: My dear Emily... Since I've won your heart, I think I have the right to call you "my dear Emily," and to kiss your fingers and your lips...

EMILY: Naughty! That's too much–and too little.

ROGER: How's that?

EMILY: You are too bold with me when we're alone, and not bold enough when my uncle is here.

ROGER: I protest.

EMILY: You promised to ask for my hand a month ago and I'm still waiting.

ROGER: I'm waiting for a favorable moment–when he's in a good mood.

EMILY: In that case, I'll be waiting for a long time, I fear.

ROGER: (*leaning forward*) My dear Emily…

EMILY: No, don't kiss me. That's bad.

ROGER: The truth is, I'm afraid he'll say no. That's why I'm hesitating.

EMILY: Ask anyway.

ROGER: But if he refuses, kicks me out, and forbids me to see you again?

EMILY: You will still have my heart.

ROGER: In that case, it's agreed. Tonight, I'll make my request!

EMILY: Tonight? Ah, my God!

ROGER: Now who's the scaredy-cat?

EMILY: Do it, Roger, and kiss me. That will give you courage.

ROGER: (*kissing her*) This is very bad, Miss Emily.

EMILY: Why, no, it's very good, Mr. Walter.

ROGER: Hush! Here's your uncle!

(*Sherlock Holmes enters.*)

EMILY: Hello, uncle.

ROGER: Hello, boss.

EMILY: (*shouting*) Mrs. Gruff, could you bring my uncle's slippers.

(*Mrs. Gruff enters, with the slippers.*)

MRS. GRUFF: Here they are, I've warmed them up.

EMILY: Good. My uncle loves to have warm feet.

ROGER: Boss, before seeing my informant, I wanted to get your instructions.

(*Holmes does not respond.*)

EMILY: Mr. Dickson stopped by earlier, uncle, but he was tired. He didn't wait for you.

(*Holmes lights his pipe as Emily sets the table.*)

ROGER: (*whispering to Emily*) He doesn't seem to be in a good mood.

EMILY: (*whispering*) Are you postponing the marriage

request?

ROGER: No. I've decided to speak and I will.

HOLMES: It's unnecessary to set a place for me. I won't be eating.

EMILY: But…

HOLMES: If you're hungry, you can eat in the office. Mrs. Gruff, earlier, I had padlocked the service entrance. Why did you remove the padlock?

MRS. GRUFF: The coal dealer came this morning, and…

HOLMES: In the future, leave locked what I lock. Is that understood?

MRS. GRUFF: (*meekly*) Yes, sir.

HOLMES: Mr. Walter and I have business here. Please leave us.

ROGER: Ah!

HOLMES: Yes, I have to speak to you.

EMILY: (*whispering to Roger*) Could he know?

ROGER: We'll soon find out.

HOLMES: Good night, Emily. Kiss me, and sleep well.

EMILY: Good night, uncle.

HOLMES: Mrs. Gruff, you will bring me a hot grog before you go to bed.

MRS. GRUFF: Would you like it right away, sir?

HOLMES: Before you retire, I said. Now run along.

(*Emily and Mrs. Gruff leave.*)

HOLMES: I have to speak to you, my lad.

ROGER: I want to speak to you as well.

HOLMES: You too? Bless me! That might be interesting. Is it on the subject of my investigation?

ROGER: Oh, no!

HOLMES: Then make it quick, so we can speak of more serious matters.

ROGER: But this is a very serious question, and strongly concerns my heart.

HOLMES: I'm listening to you; no need to beat about the bush. As for what I have to say to you, you will find out soon enough.

ROGER: Well, then, I...

HOLMES: Make it quick. We don't have all night.

ROGER: Well, certain preliminaries… I thought…

HOLMES: Be brief or we will postpone this conversation until another time.

ROGER: Very well. In a word, I love Miss Emily, and she loves me. I am formally asking you for her hand in marriage.

HOLMES: Ha! (*padding his pipe*) First of all, that wasn't a word, it was eighteen.

ROGER: What now?

HOLMES: What now? I think that, for several reasons, it would be best if you no longer came here.

ROGER: But, Mr. Holmes...

HOLMES: I was planning to reproach you, to berate you smartly. But since you've strayed to this degree, it's preferable to sever our relationship completely. Goodbye, my lad, and good luck.

ROGER: Is this a formal dismissal?

HOLMES: It seems so to me.

ROGER: I'd like an explanation first.

HOLMES: I despise speaking and saying nothing.

ROGER: All the same…

HOLMES: Enough.

ROGER: I should say it's too much.

HOLMES: For goodness sake, are you going to impose your presence on me against my will?

ROGER: I respect you as Emily's uncle, but I won't permit you to treat me as you have just done.

HOLMES: In the final analysis, what is it that you want? Emily's hand?

ROGER: Yes.

HOLMES: You shan't have it.

ROGER: Because?

HOLMES: Because. First of all, I do not have to give an account of my reasons to anyone, and certainly not to you. Furthermore, she's too young to marry. And finally, because you are an idiot.

ROGER: Excuse me?

HOLMES: An idiot. Do you understand me? And I am being polite in speaking so gently.

ROGER: What have I done to deserve such harsh words?

HOLMES: That's impudent! To dare demand Emily's hand in marriage. And ton he very evening when I discovered what I just have!

ROGER: What?

HOLMES: To think that I've worked for thirty years to establish my reputation as a consulting detective without anything having tarnished it. Then you become my secretary and catastrophes start to abound. A secretary at 120 pounds a year!

ROGER: You've never paid me.

HOLMES: I would have paid you, but not now!

(*Mrs. Gruff returns with the grog.*)

MRS. GRUFF: Here's your grog, sir.

HOLMES: Are you going to bed already?

MRS. GRUFF: No, but…

HOLMES: What did I tell you?

MRS. GRUFF: I thought…

HOLMES: You are not paid to think.

MRS. GRUFF: (*sighing*) I'll bring it back later.

HOLMES: Has Emily already gone up to her room?

MRS. GRUFF: No, sir. Miss Emily is waiting.

HOLMES: I see! She's waiting for me to reply to this buffoon. She was in league with him. Very well. You will tell her that, from now on, I Mr. Walter is forbidden to call.

ROGER: Excuse me, Mr. Holmes

HOLMES: (*turning*) Are you still here?

MRS. GRUFF: My God, my God! Poor Miss Emily!

(*She leaves.*)

ROGER: Mr. Holmes, I won't leave without knowing what I've done to deserve this. That you've refused me the hand of your niece, I can understand. But what I do not accept–what stupefies me, frankly!–is the unheard of manner in which you're treating me.

HOLMES: Since you won't leave me in peace until I've told you the reasons for my behavior, you shall know them. My response is this: First of all, what do you think of a man who doesn't keep his oath?

ROGER: I don't understand.

HOLMES: An oath upon which depends the life of a friend, and perhaps the security of the entire city of London.

ROGER: What are you getting at?

HOLMES: At this: you betrayed me, sir Probably through flightiness, perhaps unwittingly, but when one is flighty and unwitting, one can't be in the service of Sherlock Holmes, and one does not swear to absolute discretion. Because you swore that, sir.

ROGER: And I've kept my oath.

HOLMES: Now the protests of innocence begin.

ROGER: I am flabbergasted. How is it possible you could be deceived to this degree. You know men. Look into my eyes. Do I seem foolish enough to betray you, unwittingly or not, or false enough to betray you out of sheer roguery?

HOLMES: That surprised me, too. Still, my deductions accuse you, and my deductions have never been wrong.

ROGER: Explain them to me. Perhaps appearances are indeed against me, but they're only appearances. The truth is that I am innocent. We will seek out the error together.

HOLMES: Trust you again? Do you take me for a fool?

ROGER: Mr. Holmes, if I became your secretary, if I

submitted to your constant ill humor, if I risked my life a hundred times in accomplishing the perilous missions you've sent me on, it's because I love Miss Emily desperately. I swear on her head that any betrayal, knowing or unknowing, did not come from me.

HOLMES: I've had enough of your oaths.

ROGER: I thought you capable of distinguishing the true from the false.

HOLMES: You do seem sincere…

ROGER: At last!

HOLMES: …But if you are indeed innocent, then this is even more serious than I thought!

ROGER: Speak then, Master.

HOLMES: Very well, sit down, but don't imagine for a minute that you've won your case so easily. I will soon know if you have tricked me. Take care then, because that will no longer be merely unwitting, but a proof of treachery. And it will become a question of protecting my life.

ROGER: I'm listening.

HOLMES: In the last four days, I've received four warnings from Fantômas.

ROGER: Since you've been after him, you must have received many others.

HOLMES: Yes, but the last four contained more than vague threats. Each one is filled with numerous details proving that he knows everything that takes place here.

ROGER: That's amazing.

HOLMES: You know how much evidence I've gathered against this villain, and how I've succeeded in forcing him to come out of the shadows in which he lurks. He's in my power. I know the aliases with which he penetrates the diverse classes of society. I have documents proving his crimes. Finally, in two or three days, I will unmask him and deliver him to justice. Well, he knows all that. He knows all my plans.

ROGER: That's impossible!

HOLMES: This morning, I found a letter in my pocket, which said: "If you care about your life, burn all the documents you've hidden in a little black steel box."Indeed, it's in that steel box that I've locked up all the papers that accuse Fantômas. Only you, and you alone, knew that.

ROGER: But I was unaware of the greatest part of its contents. And even I don't know where you hid it.

HOLMES: Fantômas, too, is unaware of its hiding place. That's what reassures me. But still, if it's not you who has betrayed me, then who else is spying on me? Is it my niece? Young Harry Dickson? Mrs. Gruff? I've had them all followed, except for Emily, and I haven't discovered anything suspicious. But then, how does Fantômas know? How could he know? I hide everything. So, I ask myself who else... (*a pause*) Great Scott!

ROGER: What is it?

HOLMES: Look–there–on the table! Another letter from Fantômas!

ROGER: What audacity! (*picking up the letter*)

HOLMES: Read it!

ROGER: But...

HOLMES: Read it!

ROGER: (*reading*) "Mr. Holmes, you have refused to destroy the documents. I have passed your death sentence. You will die tonight at 11 p.m. Fantômas." Call everyone, question them!

HOLMES: Do you take me for a fool? Why attempt useless experiments. The one who is playing with me is very likely to betray himself this evening. All that remains for me is to await events and fight to the end.

ROGER: Let's call the Police. Do you want me to telephone them?

HOLMES: No. Can you imagine that I, who publicly boasted of exposing and ruining Fantômas, would implore the assistance and protection of Scotland Yard? That would be a farce.

ROGER: At least, allow me to stay here and help.

HOLMES: Very well. But without weapons. Until 11 p.m., I trust no one. Go bolt that door.

(*Roger bolts the door on the right.*)

ROGER: That's done.

HOLMES: The other one, too.

(*Roger bolts the second door.*)

ROGER: And the other?

HOLMES: No need. It has no exit.

(*Holmes takes one of the lamps and heads toward the door at the back*)

HOLMES: I'm going into my bedroom, which has no window, and no other door than this one. I will wait there. Don't let anyone enter.

(*Holmes leaves. There is a brief pause, then a knock on the door at the left.*)

ROGER: Someone's knocking at the door.

HOLMES: (*off from his bedroom*) Ask what they want.

ROGER: Who's there?

EMILY: (*outside*) It's me, Emily. I'm bringing the grog.

ROGER: Why isn't Mrs. Gruff bringing it?

EMILY: She's not well.

ROGER: You must take it back. Miss Emily. Your uncle doesn't want it any more.

HOLMES: (*off*) Not at all. Let her in. I am a bit thirsty.

ROGER: (*opening the door*) Then, come in, Miss Emily.

EMILY: (*entering*) I've prepared a grog for you, too, Mr. Walter. Would you like it? (*she offers him a cup*)

ROGER: (*taking the cup*) Gladly.

(*Emily goes into Holmes' bedroom. Meanwhile, Roger drinks his grog and places the empty cup on the table.*)

EMILY: (*coming back*) Good night, uncle.

HOLMES: (*off*) Until tomorrow.

EMILY: (*in a low voice to Roger*) Well?

ROGER: He refuses.

EMILY: Oh no!

(*Unseen by either Roger or Emily, the hand of Mrs. Gruff comes through the door, which is slightly ajar, and snatches the key out of the lock.*)

ROGER: But let's not be too discouraged. Perhaps he'll change his mind.

EMILY: I'll not sleep tonight.

ROGER: Courage.

EMILY: Goodnight, Roger.

(*She leaves through the door.*)

HOLMES: (*off*) Roger, don't forget to lock the door behind her.

ROGER: I'm going to... (*groping and vainly searching for the key*) The key must have fallen on the floor. I need a light...

(*Roger stumbles towards the table, on which rests the lamp by which Emily was doing her sewing earlier. His behavior indicates that he's been drugged. Finally, he reaches the table and drops into the chair. His head slumps down.*)

HOLMES: (*off*) What time is it?

ROGER: (*making an effort to sit up, looking at his watch*) Three minutes to eleven.

HOLMES Roger, my lamp is getting low. (*pause*) Roger, my lamp is out.

(*The light of the lamp in the room also goes down.*)

ROGER: Mine, too. I'm suffocating. I need air.

(*The clock strikes eleven. The lamp has now completely gone out. It is dark. From the door to the left, a man dressed all in black, his head hidden under a black hood, enters. It is Fantômas. He holds a dagger in his hand and proceeds to enter the detective's bedroom without hesitation. A silence.*)

HOLMES: (*off*) Help! I'm being attacked!

(*There is a scream.*)

ROGER: (*awakening abruptly and leaping up from the chair*) Master! I heard a call for help.

(*He goes to Holmes' door and listens.*)

ROGER: Master? (*not a sound*) Nothing! He must be asleep, just as I was… Why do I feel so sleepy? I need some air…

45

(*He goes to open the window. Meanwhile, Fantômas emerges from Holmes' room and approaches the desk. He places his bloodied dagger on it and searches for the threatening letter. Roger turns and finds himself face to face with Fantômas. Roger leaps at him.*)

ROGER: Fantômas! Then he's real! Murderer!

(*Roger grasps the dagger and tries to strike Fantômas in the chest, but his arm deviates and, instead, he pierces his hand instead.*)

ROGER: Ah, I've marked you!

(*Fantômas takes Roger by the throat and hurls him to the ground. The villain then leaves through the window, taking the letter with him.*)

EMILY: (*outside*) Mrs. Gruff! I heard my uncle scream!

(*Mrs. Gruff enters carrying a lamp in her hand, followed by Emily. Mrs. Gruff rushes into Holmes' room and soon emerges, stained with blood. She points her hand towards Roger, who is still holding the bloodied dagger.*)

MRS. GRUFF: Mr. Walter has just killed Sherlock Holmes!

(*Roger, besotted, gets up. Harry Dickson enters as Emily falls into his arms.*)

C U R T A I N

ACT II

A room in Sherlock Holmes' house. Inspector Lestrade is questioning Roger Walter.

LESTRADE: In short, you persist in your preposterous declarations!

ROGER: Because it's the truth.

LESTRADE: I cannot tell you what to say, but you must admit that your story seems implausible. A mysterious murderer, a missing key, a narcotic...

ROGER: The customary methods of Fantômas.

LESTRADE: We're going astray here. The police have already dismissed this grotesque legend.

ROGER: The murderer...

LESTRADE: We've searched the entire house; no steel box and no documents relating to this mysterious villain have been discovered. Perhaps you think that this enigmatic being also found a way to spirit those papers away by magic? With the help of fairies, perhaps?

ROGER: I beg you, Inspector, spare me your jokes. It's been ten hours and I have been the victim of the most violent emotions. I can't take it anymore. Question me, if you wish, but don't make fun of me.

47

LESTRADE: I'll question the maid now. Would you like to confront her?

(*Lestrade signals to one of his officers who introduces Mrs. Gruff.*)

MRS. GRUFF: Ah! Mr. Roger! How could you do this!

ROGER: But I'm innocent of everything, Mrs. Gruff!

LESTRADE: These lamentations are useless, woman. You must respond plainly in your own interests and those of this gentleman.

MRS. GRUFF: If it's really in your interest, I'd like to, Mr. Roger. If not, I'd prefer to say nothing.

LESTRADE: When you went in for the first time to bring a grog to Mr. Holmes, was he quarreling with Mr. Walter?

MRS. GRUFF: Well, yes, they were both shouting at each other as if they were deaf. But that's not a reason to kill someone, is it?

LESTRADE: Spare me your observations and stick to the facts, woman.

MRS. GRUFF: I think you want me to speak ill of Mr. Roger, but that won't work. I have no reasons to speak ill of him.

LESTRADE: Let's proceed in an orderly manner. According to Mr. Walter, a stranger came into the house last night. Do you see any possibility of that?

MRS. GRUFF: Does one ever know? Evil-doers are so clever these days. They can slip through the eye of a needle, if you ask me.

LESTRADE: It's a question of doors and windows, not needles.

MRS. GRUFF: Ah, by the door, it was impossible. Miss Emily will tell you that we put the chains on together.

LESTRADE: What about the rear door?

MRS. GRUFF: It was padlocked.

LESTRADE: Then, it would have been impossible for you, without Miss Emily's assistance, to open that door?

MRS. GRUFF: That's what I was going to tell you, Mr. Inspector.

LESTRADE: I will observe to you, Mr. Walter, that Mr. Dickson confirmed that, immediately after the murder, the chain was still in place on the front door, and the padlock on the rear door. What do you think of that?

ROGER: What do you expect me to think?

LESTRADE: Yes. Such details embarrass you because they plainly prove that no one could get into the house.

ROGER: But I assure you…

LESTRADE: Let's continue. Mrs. Gruff, do you know the subject of Mr. Walter and Mr. Holmes' quarrel?

MRS. GRUFF: Mr. Roger, do I still have to answer?

ROGER: Why, yes.

MRS. GRUFF: The Inspector wants to know everything because he fancies that you did the deed. As for me, I'm an honest woman, and I don't want to have your hanging on my conscience. It's better for you and for me if I say nothing.

LESTRADE: If you continue to hesitate, I am going to arrest you as an accomplice.

MRS. GRUFF: Oh, no, Mr. Inspector, don't do that. I would never survive the shame. Since I must speak, so be it. They were quarreling because Mr. Holmes had refused Mr. Roger Miss Emily's hand in marriage.

LESTRADE: Ah! Ah!

ROGER: But if we were in such bad terms, why would I have stayed with Mr. Holmes instead of leaving immediately?

LESTRADE: To settle your accounts, since you were going to be kicked out of the house.

ROGER: In that case, I would not have locked the door with the key.

LESTRADE: On the contrary, you locked the door to prevent anyone from coming to Mr. Holmes' help.

ROGER: What you said is absurd.

LESTRADE: There's more. Mrs. Gruff, do you recognize this dagger?

MRS. GRUFF: Yes, Mr. Inspector. This gentleman used it as a letter opener.

LESTRADE: Is it true?

ROGER: It is.

LESTRADE: Where was it ordinarily kept?

ROGER: In the desk drawer.

LESTRADE: And Mr. Walter frequently opened this drawer?

MRS. GRUFF: He used it in all his work. Excuse me for telling the truth, Mr. Roger, but I see there's nothing else to do.

LESTRADE: Sir, you know that it was with this dagger that the crime was committed, and you were holding the bloody weapon when Mrs. Gruff and Miss Emily rushed into the room. You do not deny it?

ROGER: I already explained that.

LESTRADE: Yes, the murderer let the dagger fall and you picked it up.

ROGER: I nailed his hand to the desk.

LESTRADE: It's regrettable that you didn't keep it in that awkward position; we would no longer doubt your sincerity for an instant.

ROGER: My strength was lacking, because of the narcotic.

LESTRADE: (*after looking at a report*) They've just examined the two glasses containing the grog.

ROGER: Well?

LESTRADE: No traces of a narcotic were found in either.

ROGER: Where did you find the glasses?

LESTRADE: Where you placed them. One on the table, the other in Mr. Holmes' room.

ROGER: We'd just drunk our grog when the same drowsiness took us both.

LESTRADE: Miss Emily prepared the drink. Are you accusing her of being in cahoots with this fantastic and imaginary Fantômas? Come, Mr. Walter, confess the truth. You acted in a moment of fury. Admit it. The jury will be fair. What's the use of denying the evidence? You can see that it's overwhelming, and against it, you submit a far-fetched fantasy that would elicit a smile from a child.

ROGER: I have nothing to confess. I'm innocent.

MRS. GRUFF: You're right to deny it, Mr. Roger. There's always time to confess when you can't do otherwise.

(*Harry Dickson enters.*)

DICKSON: Excuse me, Inspector Lestrade, but I've been dawdling behind this door for two hours. Are you going to question me soon or not?

LESTRADE: I have to leave. I won't get to you until my return, this afternoon.

DICKSON: Are you on the trail of Fantômas. I can ask you that, can't I?

LESTRADE: You, too! There is no Fantômas!

DICKSON: What?

LESTRADE: I repeat: there is no Fantômas!

DICKSON: You came to that conclusion all by yourself?

LESTRADE: Sir, you're showing a disturbing lack of respect for me.

DICKSON: Sir, you're showing a disturbing lack of respect for the evidence. For an inspector of Scotland Yard, that's a serious deficiency.

ROGER: Dickson, be careful!

DICKSON: My poor friend Mr. Holmes didn't murder himself.

ROGER: Inspector Lestrade is accusing me.

DICKSON: You? Roger Walter? You have the audacity of accusing him, Inspector Lestrade?

LESTRADE: Are you questioning me, Mr. Dickson?

DICKSON: Perish the thought! I haven't any time to waste. (*to Roger*) How could they be daft enough to accuse you of murder?

ROGER: (*glumly*) There's evidence against me.

DICKSON: What evidence? I'm sitting down, Inspector Lestrade! Surely it isn't necessary to have a brilliant intellect to see that this lad here, with his honest face and his frank eyes, is not a murderer. Come on, Inspector, take your nose out of your papers and look at reality. You will see everything much more clearly.

LESTRADE: I have to leave. (*to Roger*) I warn you frankly of the serious suspicions about you. Do not attempt to leave this house. You will be arrested by the officers watching all the exits. As for you, Mr. Dickson, I will do you the mercy of forgetting your words.

DICKSON: How generous!

LESTRADE: And you, too, are to stay here until I return.

MRS. GRUFF: Allow me to escort you out, Mr. Inspector.

LESTRADE: Consider this, Mr. Walter: it'd be better for you to confess of your own free will. Your system of defense simply won't stand up in Court.

DICKSON: And consider this, Inspector...

LESTRADE: Leave me alone, sir. I'm not speaking to you.

DICKSON: Then, allow me to escort you out, too, Inspector.

(*Lestrade, Dickson and Mrs. Gruff leave.*)

ROGER: (*alone*) Lost! I'm lost! How will I ever prove my innocence?

(*Emily enters.*)

EMILY: Roger, I've just come back from seeing my poor uncle's body. He seemed so calm. I cannot imagine that he will no longer speak. What has happened is frightful. (*weeping*)

ROGER: Perhaps it is more frightful than you imagine. Be courageous, Emily!

EMILY: Must I?

ROGER: Yes.

EMILY: What new misfortune can strike me? I will succumb to it.

ROGER: No. You will be strong.

EMILY: Tell me, what is it now?

ROGER: By this evening, I will probably be arrested.

EMILY: You! But why?

ROGER: I'm being accused of murdering your uncle.

EMILY: That's ridiculous.

ROGER: You will never believe that I'm guilty, will

you?

EMILY: Why, no one will believe it, neither the courts, nor the police.

ROGER: Don't count on it. Have you ever seen a poor fly caught in a vast spider's web? The insect vainly struggles, beats its wings, scratches with its feet. Nothing works. The more it struggles, the more it becomes enmeshed in the gluey thread, entangled on all sides. Then, the hideous spider arrives, black, voracious, sure of its prey, and the slow agony begins. I'm that fly, my poor Emily.

EMILY: That's your fate?

ROGER: The hideous, invisible Fantômas has woven a net of evidence around me that implacably hems me in. I struggle against it in vain; it's impossible to tear its fabric. He's abominably, diabolically cunning. Everything is twisted against me: my affection for you, my argument with your uncle, the precautions that we took, the weapon used for the crime.. Oh, this terrible interrogation during which I saw the evidence accumulate against me, without my being able to offer a serious objection, or refute it! I'm torturing myself to find a means of escape! But nothing! Nothing! Ah, decidedly, this Fantômas is an evil man, and he's winning every round.

EMILY: You mustn't despair. Look, a more thorough

investigation will prove the folly of the suspicions which weigh against you. Besides, you have clues to find the perpetrator: the wound you inflicted to his hand.

ROGER: Go find, among all the inhabitants of London, a man with an injured hand. No, no, all hope is lost. The documents have disappeared and unless there's a miracle, I'll be hanged.

EMILY: Don't give up! They don't hang innocent men.

ROGER: It won't be the first time.

EMILY: Then... flee.

ROGER: That would be admitting guilt.

EMILY: Since you cannot prove your innocence.

ROGER: Anyway, the police have the house surrounded. It's impossible to leave.

EMILY: They'll be put off the track. I'll find a way.

ROGER: And why should I? Wander like a hunted animal, without food, without a roof, sleeping under the stars. Unkempt, mad, wounded. No, no! I don't want that.

EMILY: You're breaking my heart.

ROGER: No! Not I! It's our invisible enemy who is taking his revenge.

(*Harry Dickson returns.*)

DICKSON: God bless me, but I'm ashamed of you, Master Walter.

ROGER: Dickson!

DICKSON: Ah, your poor employer Mr. Holmes–may God rest his soul!–was right to regard you as a pitiful detective. He saw things precisely. Does one give up in despair? Touching good-byes, death by hanging? Have you ever seen such a bedraggled chicken! You must struggle until the end, my friend. And if the game is lost, when there is nothing else to do, then you must still not give up. That's the way it is, Master Walter.

EMILY: Harry is right.

ROGER: But against the impossible…

DICKSON: The impossible! It doesn't exist? Would you like me to tell you? I would never have become Queens' boxing champion if I'd reasoned like you.

ROGER: If it was a question of physical or moral energy, I wouldn't despair. But how to struggle in the dark against a being one can't see and who strikes with treacherous blows?

DICKSON: I repeat: a pitiful detective. Come on, inspire

yourself with the example of your employer, who was the best there ever was. Ah, if you'd been murdered and he was accused, he wouldn't have any thoughts of suicide.

EMILY: Yes, defend yourself Roger–for the love of me.

DICKSON: A pair of eyes like that begs you to defend yourself, and you have no brilliant theories! No plans of counter-attack? Well? What are you going to do?

ROGER: You're both giving me such fine examples of courage that I would be ashamed not to imitate you.

EMILY: At last!

DICKSON: And none too soon!

EMILY: Let's just figure out how the murderer was able to get inside the house.

ROGER: No. First, let's try to discover how the letter signed Fantômas was placed on the desk.

DICKSON: Perhaps Fantômas was hidden in this very house.

ROGER: But who let him in? Who gave him the details of our interior? For the letters proved that the villain was well informed.

EMILY: It wasn't I.

DICKSON: Nor, I.

EMILY: Nor Mrs. Gruff.

DICKSON: Wait. Not so fast!

EMILY: You can't suspect Mrs. Gruff!

DICKSON: It's got to be one of us four.

EMILY: Mrs. Gruff is loyal to us, just like her daughter. She must have defended you, Roger, during your interrogation.

ROGER: (*after a moment's thought*) Yes, and no.

DICKSON: What does that mean?

ROGER: While ostensibly taking my side, she charged me in a terrible way. I thought it was from naivety.

DICKSON: Yeah! She's less stupid than she seems, our Mrs. Gruff...

EMILY: What then?

DICKSON: We've got the end of the thread. Now, let's unravel the ball.

EMILY: I'm beginning to hope.

DICKSON Last night, Mrs. Gruff took the padlock off

61

the rear door. The murderer was able to enter that way and hide.

EMILY: But he would have been unable to leave because I put the padlock on before the murder and kept the key in my pocket.

ROGER: That makes it incomprehensible.

EMILY: Yes. Only…

DICKSON: What?

EMILY: Mrs. Gruff bought the padlock three days ago, on the pretext that the old one wasn't working any more.

DICKSON: She could have easily procured two keys.

ROGER: That's only speculation. Let's continue. Who prepared the grog?

EMILY: Why?

ROGER: They must have contained an opiate.

EMILY: It was I who prepared them.

DICKSON: You prepared them?

EMILY: Prepared them and brought them. You remember, Roger?

ROGER: And you were not away from them for an instant?

EMILY: Not a minute.

DICKSON: (*pensively*) Where did the rum come from?

EMILY: Mrs. Gruff went to get it from the liquor cabinet.

DICKSON: Ah-ah! Does any remain in the bottle?

EMILY: No, Mrs. Gruff broke the bottle.

DICKSON: And the debris are no longer here?

EMILY: She threw them away.

ROGER: Then, she's the one who washed the glasses.

DICKSON: What?

ROGER: The Inspector told me there were no traces of an opiate in the glasses.

DICKSON: Evidently.

EMILY: Let's go inform the Inspector.

DICKSON: He'd laugh at us. These clues are enough for us, because we're convinced of Roger's innocence. They will be dismissed by the police. Let's look further.

ROGER: The dagger.

DICKSON: Yes. When the murderer entered, did he have it in his hand?

ROGER: Yes, I saw the weapon gleam.

DICKSON: Then, Mrs. Gruff must have given it to him.

ROGER: The dagger was always kept in the desk drawer —which she cleaned.

EMILY: And the lamps went out.

DICKSON: Wasn't it Mrs. Gruff who filled them?

EMILY: Always.

ROGER: What about the threatening letter placed on the desk?

EMILY: A little before you arrived, I was scolding her for rummaging through the papers on the desk.

DICKSON: And how did it vanish?

EMILY: I saw Mrs. Gruff leaning over the desk during the general excitement.

ROGER: No further doubt. Mrs. Gruff is Fantômas' accomplice.

DICKSON: Hush! Here she is!

(*Mrs. Gruff enters, carrying a bowl*.)

MRS. GRUFF: Miss Emily, I'm bringing you some bouillon. Take it, it will make you feel better.

EMILY: That's nice, Mrs. Gruff. Put it somewhere.

MRS. GRUFF: Dear Miss Emily, it will give you back all your strength. Believe in my experience as a mother.

ROGER: Leave us, Mrs. Gruff.

MRS. GRUFF: You should take something, too, Mr. Roger, it wouldn't do you any harm.

ROGER: I don't want anything.

EMILY: Tell me, Mrs. Gruff…

DICKSON: Hush!

(*There is a long, embarrassed silence*.)

MRS. GRUFF: Well, then, I'll go back to the kitchen! My God! What a terrible day...

(*Mrs. Gruff leaves*.)

DICKSON (*watching her leave*) The old bat!

EMILY: I remain puzzled. What relationship could exist between Fantômas and our old servant?

DICKSON: Are you sure that this old woman is really Margot's mother?

EMILY: What do you mean?

DICKSON: What day did you receive the first threatening letter?

ROGER: The 12th.

EMILY: And Mrs. Gruff came to replace her daughter on the 14th .

ROGER: But that letter proved Fantômas was already familiar with the activity in the house.

DICKSON: Precisely.

EMILY: Then it couldn't have been Mrs. Gruff who was spying for Fantômas.

ROGER: Unless her daughter…

DICKSON: Never. Margot is stupid, but honest.

ROGER: In that case?

DICKSON: In that case… I've got it! My friends, look at me. You have the culprit you seek before you!

ROGER and EMILY: You!

DICKSON: I was the one who betrayed you. I was the

unconscious and stupid accomplice of your enemy. I helped in the murder of Mr. Holmes and poor Margot.

ROGER and EMILY: Margot!

DICKSON: They killed your maid.

ROGER: Explain yourself.

DICKSON: You remember James Vernon?

EMILY: Your backgammon-playing friend?

ROGER: The one who abruptly vanished?

DICKSON: The same. He met with me the on the 10th. On the 11th, he met with Margot. He thought she looked sick, so he advised her to go and see Sâr Hamashkim, a seer–one of his friends.

ROGER: And she went?

DICKSON: The next day. The good fellow chatted with Margot, who was not very bright, as I said. That very night, you received your first letter.

ROGER: It's true.

DICKSON: Margot told me, "I have to go back tomorrow." She went back and never returned.

EMILY: What?

DICKSON: It was on the night of the 13th that Margot disappeared. The next day, an old woman came to say, "My daughter has fallen ill; I've come to replace her."

ROGER: Indeed!

DICKSON: You'd never seen that old woman before?

EMILY: Never.

DICKSON: Margot had never spoken of her mother?

EMILY: Truly, no!

DICKSON: That old woman was an emissary of Fantômas, introduced here to spy on you, and betray you. And to make that possible, they lured Margot into the house of Sâr Hamash-kim...

EMILY: Why, in that case, that house...

DICKSON: ...Is the lair of Fantômas!

EMILY: And you know where it is?

DICKSON: I think so. I took Margot there. They're not expecting this. They can't think of everything.

ROGER: This time, I have hope! The police will search

that house, and if they arrest a man with a pierced hand, the truth will shine forth.

EMILY: Hush! Someone's walking outside.

(*Roger goes to open the door.*)

ROGER: No one! But I hear someone walking hurriedly down the corridor. Opening the door to the street... (*calling*) Mrs. Gruff! Mrs. Gruff!

(*The street door can be heard closing.*)

ROGER: Too late! She's just left the house.

(*Emily goes to the window to take a look outside.*)

EMILY: Yes, that's Mrs. Gruff crossing the street. Where's she going?

ROGER: She must have listened at the door as we were talking.

EMILY: She's getting into a cab. She's giving the address to the driver.

DICKSON: The address of Fantômas, by Jove!

EMILY: The cab's moving fast.

ROGER: We ought to have prevented her from leaving. She's gone to warn Fantômas. The nest will be empty in an hour.

EMILY: Let's tell the police.

ROGER: The police watching us are suspicious of us.

EMILY: Let's telephone Inspector Lestrade.

DICKSON: There's nothing to be done with that bird. He'll deliberate, hesitate for hours. Fantômas will have plenty of time to get rid of the evidence and to disappear himself, since he knows our suspicions.

EMILY: Then what do we do?

DICKSON: I'm going there myself. I know the house; I'll get there before they can flee. The man who did the deed has an injured hand, right? Within an hour, I'll bring him here, dead or alive!

ROGER: You're forgetting that we're being detained here.

DICKSON: By God, that's true!

EMILY: Impossible to leave without getting yourself arrested.

DICKSON: Yet another invention of this brilliant Inspector Lestrade! He imprisons the innocent and lets the blackguards run loose.

ROGER: I have considered and taken my decision. What's the address of this so-called Sâr?

DICKSON: 47 Old Compton Street.

ROGER: I'll be there in 10 minutes. My life, my honor depend on it.

EMILY: How will you get out? The doors are all watch-ed.

DICKSON: And well watched! Two policemen at each exit.

EMILY: What if I begged them to let you pass?

ROGER: Impossible. Those men know their orders.

DICKSON: Would you like me to knock 'em out? It's only a minute's work.

ROGER: Let's think reasonably. Some trick

EMILY: Yes, but what?

ROGER: Go over the roof?

EMILY: The policemen will see you from the street and fire at you. You couldn't possibly escape that way.

ROGER: And time is passing. Mrs. Gruff will be there soon. Let's count on them taking a half hour to destroy all the compromising evidence.

DICKSON: (*looking in the back*) Hush! They're taking

Mr. Holmes' body out.

(*The sound of the dirge can be heard.*)

EMILY: Poor uncle.

DICKSON: We must think of the living. The dead are dead.

(*Two workers appear carrying an empty coffin.*)

DICKSON: Hey, friends! Don't go to the first floor. Come in here with your burden! Yes, the stiff is up there, but stop here. Put the coffin down and listen to me. You'd normally earn five shillings today. Well, I will give you 500. All I have.

EMILY: Mister Dickson!

ROGER: I will not allow...

DICKSON: Peace! (*to the workers*) I will give you 25 pounds if you will carry the coffin through the service door you see there– just opposite. Only there will be someone else in it. Come on, don't hesitate. It's a unique opportunity. No one will suspect anything. You will save an innocent man and make me a happy man. What do you say?

(*The two workers look at each other, then nod, grunting their approval.*)

DICKSON: Come on, into the coffin, Roger. The corridor is dark and the house has two exits. You understand the rest. Good luck!

(*Roger gets into the coffin.*)

EMILY: Courage!

ROGER: Don't worry. In an hour, Fantômas will be caught.

EMILY: Here's my uncle's revolver.

ROGER: Thank you.

DICKSON: (*to the workers*) Now close the coffin. There. I am giving you a pat of the hand. It's heavy, huh? That means nothing. Your billfold will be the perfect a counter-weight. You make a sign from across the street when the escape has been carried out. Be careful now.

(*The workers leave with the coffin.*)

DICKSON: (*pretending to talk to Roger, shouting on the stairway so that the police on guard will hear him*) Your boss was stupid, my friend. He should have been more careful.

EMILY: Are they letting the coffin through?

DICKSON: Hush! (*to a policeman, off*) Hallo, Mr. Bobby. Does it amuse you to stand guard before our door? Say then, you aren't very polite, are you? You could answer me.

EMILY: Well?

DICKSON: (*shutting the door*) Go look out the window, and if they've crossed without difficulties.

(*She does so.*)

EMILY: Yes. They're staggering under the weight. The police are watching them. Are they going to suspect anything?

DICKSON: Come on! Come on!

EMILY: They're going under a coach door. They've disappeared.

DICKSON: It's going fine!

EMILY: The worker has reappeared. He's giving the agreed signal. Roger must have won his freedom. Saved!

DICKSON: Saved! That old swine Fantômas is going to spend a bad quarter of an hour!

CURTAIN

ACT III

A cellar. There is a table with a telephone on it, whimsical furniture of all types, and a buffet at the back. To the left of the audience, there is a stairway-ramp with steps leading to a door. It is night.

FANTÔMAS: (*outside*) Go in. I'm waiting.

VACHARD: (*appearing, lighting a pocket lamp*) Inside here?

FANTÔMAS: (*still outside*) Yes, go down.

VACHARD: (*stumbling*) I'll never get used to these steps.

FANTÔMAS: That's tough!

VACHARD: I'm afraid of breaking my leg. When you go from daylight to this dark hole, you can't see a thing.

FANTÔMAS: (*appearing at the top of the stairs*) If it will make you happy, I'll replace the walls with glass.

VACHARD: One would see better. And that would be useful to lots of folks.

FANTÔMAS: You think you're funny?

(*Vachard lights a lantern.*)

VACHARD: No, I'm making light of the situation.

FANTÔMAS: (*coming down*) Very droll!

VACHARD: I always feel depressed when I have to leave warm sunlight and a beautiful ceremony.

FANTÔMAS: Yes. Everyone there was choice.

VACHARD: You can say that again. And especially fruitful.

FANTÔMAS: (*removing his gloves*) Did you steal anything?

(*Fantômas' right hand is bandaged.*)

VACHEROT: Hardly anything. Just enough to pay our expenses.

FANTÔMAS: (*stern*) Vachard, I will never take you into London society again.

VACHARD: I can't help it. I don't like wasting my time.

FANTÔMAS: Is it wasting your time to check out a mansion that you'll clean out in two weeks?

VACHARD: I've taken a few things on account.

FANTÔMAS: As Dr. Garrick, I was the one invited to

the marriage of Lord Ascott, and I introduced you as my French cousin to all present. But if they'd caught you red-handed, what would they have thought of me?

VACHARD: They would have asked you if I was training to be a politician, heh, heh.

FANTÔMAS: Enough! Don't let it happen again. I sometimes need an auxiliary in society. As you present well, I us you, but try to forget your old profession as a pickpocket. I've made you my lieutenant. Make yourself worthy of my confidence.

VACHARD: I promise you, Master.

FANTÔMAS: (*sitting*) Now show me your swag.

VACHARD: Ah, do I have to?

FANTÔMAS: Of course.

VACHARD: It's barely worth the trouble…

FANTÔMAS: Come on.

VACHARD: Here!

(*He pulls some jewels from his pocket.*)

FANTÔMAS: Is that all?

VACHARD: Yes. (*a pause*) Er, no, there's this too. (*giv-*

ing more)

FANTÔMAS: (*dividing the loot*) Here's your share.

VACHARD: (*disappointed*) Thanks.

FANTÔMAS: Now, let's talk business. Have you received the report of last night's expeditions?

VACHARD: Yes, Master.

FANTÔMAS: I'm listening.

VACHARD: Lambert and his crew worked at Russell House.

FANTÔMAS: The result?

VACHARD: The furniture is in our store room. Here are the jewels. (*handing over a black case*)

FANTÔMAS: I'll examine them soon.

VACHARD: I gave 500 pounds to Lambert on account.

FANTÔMAS: Perfect. The receipt?

VACHARD: Here, Master.

FANTÔMAS: Any bodies?

VACHARD: The old Baron and a flunkey. On your orders, they spared the dog.

FANTÔMAS: You must never harm animals! What next?

VACHARD: Gilmore bungled his job.

FANTÔMAS: Ah!

VACHARD: He was supposed to do the home of the Director of the Midlands Bank. The servants were awakened while he was forcing a lock.

FANTÔMAS: Clumsy.

VACHARD: During his escape, he dropped his hat.

FANTÔMAS: I don't like this at all. You tell him I am very displeased.

VACHARD: Yes, Master.

FANTÔMAS: Is that all?

VACHARD: No. Baron Rollison placed the ransom in the place indicated. Here's the money. In bearer's bonds, as requested. (*handing him a folder*)

FANTÔMAS: That dear man. It made him ill, I'm sure. That's why we didn't see him at the wedding this morning... Did we get our letters back?

VACHARD: His servant, who is one of us, brought them to me this morning.

FANTÔMAS: Has he been paid?

VACHARD: Fifty pounds. Here's the receipt.

FANTÔMAS: What's Turnbull doing right now?

VACHARD: He's awaiting your instructions.

FANTÔMAS: For some time now, he's been mostly getting drunk, and has started to speak more than necessary. This must stop...

VACHARD: I'll tell him.

FANTÔMAS: No. That would be useless. I shall have *to cut the branch*. Invite him for a glass of whiskey and pour this into it.

(*Fantômas pulls a small flask from his pocket which he hands to Vachard.*)

VACHARD: But...

FANTÔMAS: Do you have an objection?

VACHARD: (*cowed*) None, Master. Shall I do it here, or down there?

FANTÔMAS: It doesn't matter. Wherever the opportunity presents itself. The rest is your concern. I never want to see him again. It's a shame. Turnbull was a very good lad, very devoted to the Brotherhood–but weak. His end will serve as a lesson. Is that all?

VACHARD: Yes, Master.

FANTÔMAS: While we're on the subject of disappear-
ances, what about this maid of Holmes'
whom I delivered to you several days ago?

VACHARD: The lime kiln has done its work. Nothing
remains except ashes.

FANTÔMAS: This Holmes business is causing me some
anxiety.

VACHARD: What worries you now that he's dead?

FANTÔMAS: That chance will reveal the box of documents that I was unable to secure.

VACHARD: To think that Mrs. Gruff was never able to
learn where Holmes hid it.

FANTÔMAS: That's unforgivable.

VACHARD: On the other hand, the police haven't
found it either.

FANTÔMAS: It's the job of Scotland Yard to be stupid.
What would become of us if they weren't?

VACHARD: Which reminds me, I have to deliver this to
you on behalf of Mrs. Gruff. (*handing him a
key*)

FANTÔMAS: A key?

VACHARD: She took it last night from Holmes' neck.

FANTÔMAS: This is surely the key to the documents box. Now only the box itself is missing. I will go and look for it myself.

FANTÔMAS: How will you be able to find it?

FANTÔMAS: I don't know, but I must get those documents! My work is only half done. Roger Walter will *pay the law* and hang for Holmes' murder. That's not bad. But the documents that Holmes gathered still exist. They expose my various identities: Tom Bob, Dr. Garrick... Their discovery can compromise everything.

VACHARD: Why expose yourself, Master? Mrs. Gruff is continuing her investigation. Or you could send someone trustworthy: me, for example. I'm in good with young Harry Dickson, who only knows me as his friend James Vernon. My presence will be easily explained.

FANTÔMAS: I'll send you there, but I have enough at stake in this matter to personally put my hand in the pot. I'll continue to take care of it personally.

VACHARD: That could cost you dear, Master.

FANTÔMAS: (*looking at his injured hand*) It's already cost me. But what does it matter?

VACHARD: Will you give your consultations as the Sâr Hamashkim today?

FANTÔMAS: What time is it?

VACHARD: Two o'clock.

FANTÔMAS: Any clients?

VACHARD: A dozen.

FANTÔMAS: I'll see them.

VACHARD: With the outfit? The wig?

FANTÔMAS: Yes. These consultations are my main daily distraction. You cannot imagine, Vachard, how it amuses me to make these fools tell me where they've hidden their money, while reading the lines of their hands or prescribing some herbs for their rheumatism.

VACHARD: I leave magic and palm reading to you, Master, but as far as rheumatism is concerned, God bless me, if you don't treat them well...

FANTÔMAS: You're a fool, Vachard. It's all in the mind. For a price, all the clients of the old Sâr Hamashkim bring so much information to Fantômas.

(*Mrs. Gruff enters abruptly.*)

MRS. GRUFF: Master, pardon me.

FANTÔMAS: What is the meaning of this, Mrs. Gruff? You dare come here without my permission?

MRS. GRUFF: I have reason.

FANTÔMAS: Do you?

MRS. GRUFF: It's serious.

FANTÔMAS: It's even more serious to disobey my orders. Don't you know that?

MRS. GRUFF: Forgive me, Master!

FANTÔMAS: Enough! For this time, I will pardon you. But if you ever do it again… What do you have to tell me?

MRS. GRUFF: We've been discovered. Roger Walter and Harry Dickson have found out the truth; they know that the seer Sâr Hamashkim and Fantômas are the same person.

FANTÔMAS: Have they informed Lestrade?

MRS. GRUFF: No. They're afraid he won't take them seriously.

FANTÔMAS: Not badly reasoned.

MRS. GRUFF: Walter intends to come here himself to

surprise you.

FANTÔMAS: Really!

MRS. GRUFF: Lestrade forbade him to leave the house,
but I'm sure Dickson will find a way for him
to get out, and he'll be here any moment
now.

FANTÔMAS: Very interesting.

MRS. GRUFF: Unfortunately, you can't make him disappear. Dickson is aware of the plan and
would inform Scotland Yard.

FANTÔMAS: Is that all?

MRS. GRUFF: Flee, Master! I beg you, flee! Your life is
in danger.

VACHARD: Permit me to join my voice to that of Mrs.
Gruff. We are your two most faithful lieutenants.

MRS. GRUFF: I've known you since you were a child,
being raised by that old crook, Paterson. I
have nothing but affection for you! Listen to
me.

VACHARD: Since this wiring allows us to blow up the
house, let's seek refuge in our cellars in Ox-
ford Street, and make this box collapse. All
the evidence piled up here will vanish with
one stroke.

MRS. GRUFF: Believe me, it's for the best.

FANTÔMAS: Enough! I pardon you because you love me, but you're going too far.

VACHARD: But…

FANTÔMAS: If you're afraid, you can flee.

VACHARD: We'll stay, right, Mrs. Gruff?

MRS. GRUFF: Yes, Master.

FANTÔMAS: Fine. How many men do you have at hand?

VACHARD: Three.

FANTÔMAS: That's more than are needed. All enter at the usual signal.

(*ringing*)

FANTÔMAS: Someone's at the door. Let him in and send away the other visitors.

MRS. GRUFF: Master!

FANTÔMAS: You're starting to bother me, Mrs. Gruff. You will come at my first call, not before. Now, go!

(*Mrs. Gruff and Vachard leave. Alone, Fantômas puts*

on a wig and oriental robes and a turban. Then he goes to sit behind a table. Roger Walter enters.)

ROGER: Excuse me, sir, are you Sâr Hamashkim?

FANTÔMAS: Yes. To whom have I the honor of speaking?

ROGER: My visit to you was not announced by the spirits?

FANTÔMAS: I need to know your name in order to respond.

ROGER: I thought you would have guessed it.

FANTÔMAS: There are things that remain hidden, even to seers such as I. But we are speaking of the mysteries of the universe.

ROGER: Isn't that a natural topic, for such a powerful and formidable seer as yourself?

FANTÔMAS: You flatter me, sir. Have you come to consult my science about something in particular?

ROGER: Yes.

FANTÔMAS: Very well. Sit down and give me your hand.

ROGER: Here it is. (*extending his hand*)

FANTÔMAS: A beautiful hand. Energetic, but unlucky.

ROGER: How true.

FANTÔMAS: May I say something troubling?

ROGER: By all means.

FANTÔMAS: I see death in your hand. Death, after a brief interval.

ROGER: Ah!

FANTÔMAS: It would be more agreeable to me to announce a happy love, an approaching marriage, or struggles crowned with success. Alas, all I see is defeat.

ROGER: Are you sure?

FANTÔMAS: Very sure.

ROGER: Your science must deceive you. For very recently, Fate appears to have favored me.

FANTÔMAS: A common mistake. Destiny seems to favor you, the better to ruin you. Resign yourself. I tell you that your hand predicts impending death, or at least a shameful defeat.

ROGER: You are not very reassuring for a fortune-teller.

FANTÔMAS: I am only the interpreter of Fate!

ROGER: Sometimes, one has to give Fate a solid kick in the posterior.

FANTÔMAS: That remains to be seen.

ROGER: But what if the victim fights back?

FANTÔMAS: That's quite difficult to do.

ROGER: Is that all you read in my hand?

FANTÔMAS: I read a host of things, even more terrifying. You are surrounded by terrible enemies.

ROGER: I know who they are.

FANTÔMAS: So do I. And what is distressing for you is that they will defeat you. You have a very unfortunate hand, sir.

ROGER: But at least, it's not cut like yours–Fantômas!

(*With an abrupt gesture, he removes the bandage from Fantômas' hand, exposing the wound. He then pulls out his gun and points it toward Fantômas.*)

ROGER: Not a shout, not a gesture, or I will blow you away.

FANTÔMAS: Damn it!

ROGER: At last, before my eyes, I have the invincible Fantômas. Here you are: unmasked and ready to be arrested!

FANTÔMAS: You look arrogant in your triumph, Mr. Walter.

ROGER: And you, pitiful in your defeat.

FANTÔMAS: You might have spared hurting me by not tearing the dressing from my wounded hand.

ROGER: That's only a preview of what the executioner has in store for you.

FANTÔMAS: What a cruel soul you have.

ROGER: Don't try any swaggering. You can see plainly that you've lost. I've got you here, pale with fear.

FANTÔMAS: You were wrong to ignore the warnings I saw in the lines of your hand.

(*Fantômas lets out a sharp whistle and abruptly extinguishes the lights. Complete darkness. Vachard, aided by three men, rush Roger Walter and tie him to the post at the end of the stairs.*)

ROGER: (*struggling*) Wretches! Wretches!

FANTÔMAS: Tie him carefully... Fine.

(*Mrs. Gruff relights the lamps. The other three bandits leave at a gesture from Fantômas.*)

VACHARD: Should we electrocute him, Master?

FANTÔMAS: I'm considering.

VACHARD: He's a dangerous witness. His death is required for our safety.

ROGER: Kill me, then. Harry Dickson knows where to find me and will avenge me.

VACHARD: Childish threats.

FANTÔMAS: I wonder…

VACHARD: Please allow me to press the button that will dispatch him to the next world.

FANTÔMAS: No. His life is still necessary. Put a gag on him. Vachard, you will pay a visit to Mr. Dickson…

VACHARD: Yes, Master.

FANTÔMAS: (*to Roger*) Well, my friend, don't you think I knew the future better than you now? To try to catch Fantômas in his own lair! Heavens, I'd pity you if, besides being stupid, you were not also so pretentious. Ah, your employer, the great Mr. Holmes, was forged of a different mettle. With him, at least, I fenced. With you, I play. Still, you came here unexpectedly, you've cost me some annoyance and disarray. But I'm not complaining. You will be very useful, my friend, very useful... I'm so grateful to you, in fact, that I intend to let you live and restore your freedom. Don't be impatient. Learn to wait. Have no fear that I will not keep my promise. Fantômas always keeps his word. Mrs. Gruff, what is the telephone number at Sherlock Holmes' residence?

MRS. GRUFF: 88-22, Master.

FANTÔMAS: Right. (*taking the telephone*) Hello! Hello! 88-22. (*covering the speaker with his hand*) Mrs. Gruff, hand me Mr. Walter's wallet, will you? (*into the telephone*) Who is this? Miss Emily? (*to Mrs. Gruff*) Mrs. Gruff, make sure he's still well gagged.

MRS. GRUFF: He is, Master.

(*She hands him a wallet she took from Roger's breast pocket.*)

FANTÔMAS: (*into the telephone*) Emily! It's me, Roger. Oh! Pay no attention; my voice is trembling with emotion. Fantômas will be arrested in a few moments. I found that we wrongly accused Mrs. Gruff. She is very honest, entirely trustworthy. It's thanks to her that I've been able to unmask the wretch. I'll tell you everything when I return. But let's talk of more pressing things. The police are here; they need your testimony. So I'm sending Mrs. Gruff to get you. She'll come in a taxi. What! You doubt me? Don't you

92

recognize my voice? Here's proof that it is really me, Roger, who is speaking to you. Do you recognize this letter? (*taking a letter from Roger's wallet*) "My dear Roger, all night I've thought about you and a thousand things went through my head; but now that I want to write you…" Ah, you believe me at last! Good! I approve of you being cautious. So many dangers surround us. And to reassure you completely, I'll give Mrs. Gruff the gold ring I wear on my finger… (*gesturing to Mrs. Gruff*)

(*Mrs. Gruff removes the ring from Roger's finger.*)

FANTÔMAS: So it's agreed? I am sending Mrs. Gruff, and you are to accompany her. See you soon, my darling. We are saved.

(*He hangs up the telephone.*)

FANTÔMAS: Mrs. Gruff, you may remove the gag from Mr. Walter, which must surely annoy him.

(*She does as instructed.*)

FANTÔMAS: You understand the plan, Mrs. Gruff? Once in the car, you will tell the girl a yarn– it doesn't matter what–and take her to our main office and lock her up in the padded room. Now, listen carefully. I will come in person for her before 10 p.m. If at 10 p.m. exactly, I haven't returned, then you will kill

93

her slowly, in such a way that it will take her 12 hours to die. She should expire by around 10 a.m. the next morning.

ROGER: My God! This is a dreadful nightmare!

FANTÔMAS: My orders will be executed.

MRS. GRUFF: To the letter, Master.

ROGER: Mrs. Gruff! If you have a human soul, so much as a little heart, please, don't be so cruel.

FANTÔMAS: You can leave, Mrs. Gruff.

ROGER: Mrs. Gruff! Please!

(*Mrs. Gruff leaves, unmoved.*)

FANTÔMAS: There's only one creature here with a human heart, Mr. Walter, and that's me. The others are not human, but instruments at the service of our Brotherhood, and such instruments have no soul.

ROGER: What is the purpose of this horrible blackmail?

FANTÔMAS: Vachard, go watch Holmes' house and come tell me if Mrs. Gruff succeeds in carrying the girl off.

(*Vachard leaves.*)

FANTÔMAS: Mr. Walter, Mr. Holmes' house isn't far from here. Mrs. Gruff will probably escort your fiancée out any moment now.

ROGER: What then?

FANTÔMAS: The best detectives in all of London will never discover our hideout. I, alone, can save her.

ROGER: What do you want?

FANTÔMAS: I have a question for you. Answer truthfully. Any lie on your part would be extremely dangerous for you, and your fiancée.

ROGER: I'm listening.

FANTÔMAS: Have you communicated this address to Scotland Yard?

ROGER: No.

FANTÔMAS: What about Harry Dickson?

ROGER: I don't think he has. But it's obvious he will, if he doesn't see me return.

FANTÔMAS: That's what I want to avoid. It's not convenient for me to have them come and ransack this place.

ROGER: You can't prevent it.

FANTÔMAS: I think I can. Or more precisely, you will do it for me.

ROGER: I?

FANTÔMAS: Yes. You will return to Baker Street and tell Dickson that your suspicions were ill founded, that you found nothing suspect here, that the Sâr Hamashkim is merely an old fraud... In short, you will prevent the young American from informing Scotland Yard.

ROGER: Inspector Lestrade will arrest me if I go back there.

FANTÔMAS: Have no fear; you'll be watched.

ROGER: Then how do you want me to prove my innocence?

FANTÔMAS: I don't want you to do that.

ROGER: You don't want me to?

FANTÔMAS: They must all believe you guilty, so that all this talk about Fantômas will stop.

ROGER: Don't count on it! You can kill me, but I won't dishonor myself by collaborating in your evil schemes!

FANTÔMAS: It's not you that I will kill: it's your fiancée. Slowly.

ROGER: My God!

FANTÔMAS: Come on, save this poor child who loves you so much, and who doesn't deserve to die in such an agonizing manner.

ROGER: Her life will be spared if I obey you?

FANTÔMAS: Yes.

ROGER: What will guarantee that?

FANTÔMAS: My word! Fantômas keeps his word in good and in evil, always.

ROGER: I will obey you.

FANTÔMAS: You'd better…

(*Vachard returns.*)

VACHARD: Holmes' niece is secure, Master.

FANTÔMAS: Perfect! Cut this gentleman loose.

ROGER: Oh!

FANTÔMAS: No nerves! Go fulfill your promise, and don't forget that everywhere, there's an eye on you. Not one suspicious look, not a hint of betrayal or Miss Emily is lost. Until ten o'clock, I'm placing myself in your hands.

ROGER: At ten o'clock, you'll set her free?

FANTÔMAS: Keep your word and I will keep mine.

(*Roger goes slowly up the stairs.*)

FANTÔMAS: You can leave, Mr. Walter. Didn't I predict that you were headed for defeat? Don't forget it. If your fiancée dies tonight, an atrocious death, you'll be the one who killed her.

(*Roger leaves.*)

CURTAIN

ACT IV

Later, at Sherlock Holmes' Baker Street residence. The décor is the same as Act I.

VACHARD: No more policemen at the door? I can risk it.

(He goes to the door on the left and looks through the keyhole.)

VACHARD: Ah, there's my dear friend, Harry Dickson! This couldn't be better. We're playing for high stakes indeed.

(Roger Walter enters.)

VACHARD: Remember your promise, sir–if you want my master to keep his.

ROGER: Is Inspector Lestrade in the house?

VACHARD: That, I don't know. But Dickson is over there, alone. You must talk to him and make sure he no longer believes that Sâr Hamash-kim is Fantômas.

ROGER: What should I say?

VACHARD: Whatever you please. Just prevent him from telling Scotland Yard. Your fiancée's life is at stake.

ROGER: I'll do it.

VACHARD: Remember, don't attempt to betray us. I'll be here to keep an eye on you.

ROGER: What if Dickson sees you?

VACHARD: Are we not great friends? He'll be delighted to see his old pal James Vernon who paid for all his drinks and played backgammon with him.

ROGER: He suspects you.

VACHARD: It's up to you to destroy all his suspicions.

ROGER: Here he is.

(*Harry Dickson enters, looking very thoughtful.*)

VACHARD: Harry! My old pal, how are you?

DICKSON: You! (*aside*) What's he doing here?

VACHARD: I learned of this terrible murder and...

ROGER: Dickson, I...

DICKSON: Roger! You're back! Has Fantômas been arrested?

ROGER: We were on the wrong track. The Sâr Hamashkim isn't Fantômas.

DICKSON: Why did you telephone then? Why did Mrs. Gruff come to take Miss Emily away?

ROGER: I thought I'd catch the murderer, but I was wrong. You'll learn all about it later. Right now, I'm too tired to explain everything to you.

DICKSON: Where's Emily?

ROGER: I didn't see her. We must have missed each other. She'll be back any minute.

DICKSON: Why did you come back, then? To get arrested?

ROGER: I came to tell you to not disturb the Sâr. He's innocent.

DICKSON: And that's the only reason?

ROGER: I also wanted to know if Emily had actually gone out.

DICKSON: Obviously, she's gone out. (*aside*) This is all very strange. (*pointing to Vachard*) What are you doing with this gentleman?

VACHARD: I haven't had the honor of meeting him yet. I've just met him here by chance.

DICKSON: You might have left him the trouble of lying for himself. He's got a tongue, hasn't he? Anyway, since you claim you don't know

101

each other... (*introducing them*) This is my famous backgammon playing buddy, James Vernon… And this is Roger Walter, accused of murder by Scotland Yard.

VACHARD: You, sir, a murderer? I'm sure that's not the case. I hope the truth will soon shine forth, and you will be completely exonerated.

DICKSON: I hope so, too. (*aside*) Roger is innocent, and yet they're conniving together. Why? (*aloud*) Do you know, Roger, that Inspector Lestrade is here? He's searching the upper floors. Do you still want to get arrested?

ROGER: Yes–no. I'm undecided.

DICKSON: (*aside*) I see! He's checking what he should say with the other one. I must speak to him alone. (*aloud*) As for you, James, what are you doing here?

VACHARD: As I said, I heard about the murder and came to take you out for a pint.

DICKSON: Wait for me at the corner's pub then. I'll join you shortly.

VACHEROT: But…

DICKSON: I said, I'll join you. You were quite capable of spending a week without me, and we'll only be separated for a quarter of an hour. That should be quite bearable.

(*Fantômas enters.*)

FANTÔMAS: It seems that anyone can walk in here.

DICKSON: Who are you, sir?

FANTÔMAS: (*offering him his card*) My card...

DICKSON: (*reading*) Detective Tom Bob. (*aside*) He looks intelligent.

FANTÔMAS: Is Inspector Lestrade here?

DICKSON: Yes, sir. He's upstairs conducting a search.

FANTÔMAS: Would you be so kind as to take me to him?

DICKSON: I'd rather inform him of your arrival.

FANTÔMAS: In that case, please deliver this letter to him.

DICKSON: With pleasure. (*aside*) I wouldn't want to leave Roger alone with Vernon, but now that someone from the Yard is here, I feel more comfortable.

(*Dickson leaves.*)

FANTÔMAS: (*to Vachard*) So, has Mr. Walter kept his word? Harry Dickson no longer suspects us?

VACHARD: I hope not. But his explanations have been rather pitiful, and if it wasn't for my presence here, he certainly would have betrayed us.

FANTÔMAS: You shouldn't have stopped him. If he chooses to kill his fiancée, that's his business.

ROGER: In the end, I've kept my word. Will you keep yours?

FANTÔMAS: It's not 10 p.m. yet, sir.

ROGER: What do I have to do?

FANTÔMAS: Await my further orders.

ROGER: Where?

FANTÔMAS: Here.

ROGER: But the police will see me and arrest me. It's already a miracle that I'm still free.

VACHARD: An hour sooner, an hour later...

ROGER: But it's true, since I'm destroying the evidence of my innocence myself.

VACHARD: Love is stronger than honor! Now, there's a good title for a pulp novel!

FANTÔMAS: Vachard, see if Lestrade…

VACHARD: He's upstairs. We'll hear him when he comes down.

FANTÔMAS: Have they already searched the cellar?

VACHARD: Probably.

FANTÔMAS: Good! So the Inspector won't descend any further. Anyway, I'll prevent that. No one is likely to disturb us?

VACHARD: (*half-opening the door*) No, MASTER.

FANTÔMAS: (*to Roger*) Sit at the desk and write: "I, Roger Walter, confess to being the murderer of my employer, Mr. Sherlock Holmes. I choose to kill myself in remorse."

ROGER: What?

FANTÔMAS: Must I always repeat that I don't want you to question my orders? Don't worry. I'm not thinking of killing you. But think of Emily before you make up your mind.

(*Roger sits down and writes the letter.*)

FANTÔMASL Sign it ! Fine.   (*pocketing the letter*) Now go hide in the cellar.

(*Roger leaves.*)

VACHARD: Why are you making him stay?

FANTÔMAS: He must be at my disposal in case things go wrong.

VACHARD: There was no need for you to expose yourself by coming here.

FANTÔMAS: Could I risk seeing the documents which reveal all my secrets falling into the hands of Scotland Yard? No! I must be here to find them, or seize them in the event they're discovered.

VACHARD: What will my role be in all this?

FANTÔMAS: Your friendship with Dickson more or less explains your presence here. Don't go far.

VACHARD: Would you like me to search as well?

FANTÔMAS: They might surprise you and that would complicate matters.

(*Dickson returns.*)

DICKSON: (*aside*) Heavens! Roger has left! And those two look pretty cozy to me.

FANTÔMAS: Well, sir?

DICKSON: Inspector Lestrade read your letter. He's coming.

FANTÔMAS: Thank you.

(*Lestrade enters holding a steel box.*)

LESTRADE: Detective Tom Bob, right?

FANTÔMAS: Will you do as I requested?

LESTRADE: I've heard much about you, sir. You're said to belong to the Council of Five. The authorization you want from me isn't orthodox, but between colleagues, we shouldn't refuse each other such a service. I'm at your disposal.

FANTÔMAS: I don't know how to thank you.

LESTRADE: It's nothing. This crime seems much more mysterious than I first imagined. I discovered this steel box behind a panel. Perhaps it will provide us with the key to the mystery.

FANTÔMAS: You haven't opened it?

LESTRADE: No, the key appears to be missing.

FANTÔMAS: (*aside*) Luckily, I have it.

LESTRADE: But I've got a locksmith coming. He should be here any minute. Now I have to finish our search.

FANTÔMAS: Will you allow me to accompany you?

LESTRADE: By all means.

FANTÔMAS: Are you taking the box with you?

LESTRADE: Why, yes.

FANTÔMAS: But that will needlessly encumber you. Shall we leave it here, under the watch of these gentlemen?

LESTRADE: I would rather call one of my officers.

FANTÔMAS: Why? (*pointing to Vachard*) He's one of my most trusted assistants.

LESTRADE: In that case… (*giving the steel box to Vachard*) Hold on to this.

FANTÔMAS: (*low to Vachard, handing him as key*) Here's the key. Empty it for me.

(*Lestrade leaves, followed by Fantômas.*)

DICKSON: (*aside*) This Tom Bob isn't from Scotland Yard. He and Vernon are in cahoots together.

VACHARD: By the way, Dickson, your young friend just went down to the cellar. He asked me to tell you he wanted to see you.

DICKSON: Did he now?

VACHARD: He has something important to tell you.

DICKSON: I see.

VACHARD: Go on, he's waiting for you.

DICKSON: Shut up! I'm thinking, I'm considering.

VACHARD: Considering what?

DICKSON: Our supposed old friendship.

VACHARD: "Supposed"? That's not very nice.

DICKSON: Isn't it?

VACHARD: In any event, we've only known each other for two weeks.

DICKSON: Indeed. All the same, we were quite a pair of friends, weren't we?

VACHARD: Yes we were.

DICKSON: Every day, we played a game of backgammon together.

VACHARD: (*aside*) Will he never leave? I'll open the damned box anyway.

(*Vachard tries to open the box with the key.*)

DICKSON: And how many drinks you bought me…

VACHARD: Yes, yes, but Mr. Walter's waiting for you.

DICKSON: And yet, I haven't offered you anything in

return. That's rather ungentlemanly of me.

VACHARD: Go talk to him. His freedom might depend on your intervention.

DICKSON: I didn't pay for any drinks, not one single time.

VACHARD: You can buy me one later. Don't worry about it. Go!

DICKSON: Right, later. Well, I'm going to be repaying you all your favors, my dear Vernon...

VACHARD: You know, there's really no need to.

(*Vachard unlocks the box.*)

DICKSON: ...With interest. (*rolling up his sleeves*)

VACHARD: What–what are you doing?

DICKSON: I insist! (*delivering a formidable punch to Vachard*) Here's a first installment!

VACHARD: Are you mad? What are...?

DICKSON: No, I see you for what you are! Second in-stallment. Cash only. Boom! (*punching him in the teeth*).

VACHARD: (*pulling out a knife*) Stop hitting me, you damn Yankee, r...

DICKSON: Come on, James, old pal, we shouldn't play with knives… (*disarming him*) That could be dangerous. (*keeps punching Vachard whose face ends up all covered with blood*) One last round, shall we?

VACHARD: Stop! Please!

(*Vachard collapses on the floor, on top of the box.*)

DICKSON: Have you had enough?

(*Fantômas returns.*)

FANTÔMAS: What's been going on here? What happened to this man?

DICKSON: Pay no attention to him, sir. We had a minor disagreement about of round of drinks.

FANTÔMAS: It's ridiculous, sir, to suggest that a "minor disagreement," as you put it, would lead to someone ended up in such a state. Mr. Vernon, get up!

VACHARD: I… I…

(*Vachard gets up, abandoning the box on the floor.*)

DICKSON: (*laughing, to Vachard*) Yes, I quite agree, it's ridiculous, sir, to end up in such a state!

FANTÔMAS: (*to Vachard*) Go wash your face. It looks terrible.

VACHARD: (*muttering at Dickson*) Bastard! You'll pay for this!

(*Vachard leaves. Fantômas has noticed the box and slowly moves forward with the intention of taking it. But Dickson has observed his maneuvering. As Fantômas bends over to pick it up, the young American places his foot on the box. Fantômas, vexed, moves away. Dickson then grasps the box and places it safely under his arm.*)

DICKSON: It has been a pleasure making your acquaintance, sir.

(*He takes Fantômas' hand, his wounded hand, and squeezes it with all his strength.*)

FANTÔMAS: (*screaming dully*) Aie!

DICKSON: (*aside*) My, my! His hand is very sensitive. (*aloud*) Excuse me, I'm going to take this back to Inspector Lestrade.

FANTÔMAS: But...

DICKSON: (*looking at him fixedly*) I am taking this back to the Inspector.

(*He leaves.*)

FANTÔMAS: (*drawing his revolver, then changing his mind*) No, that would make too much noise. Still, I must have that box. Vachard!

(*Vachard returns.*)

VACHARD: I'm here!

FANTÔMAS: I ordered you to empty that box.

VACHARD: It's done.

FANTÔMAS: What?

VACHARD: My eyes may look like black butter, and my ribs are sore, but here are the documents. I took them when I was crouching over the box. (*handing some papers*)

FANTÔMAS: At last! Lestrade won't return too soon. Go fetch Walter.

(*Exit Vachard.*)

FANT^OMAS: (*alone, going through the papers*) Damn! If the police had discovered them, I would have been ruined. Description. Threatening letters. Aliases. Addresses. That devil Sherlock Holmes had everything. It was a bomb ready to burst at any moment. Well, now it won't. It will sputter like a wet fire-cracker. Well, Sherlock Holmes, did I beat you or not? You perished by my hand. Your niece is in my power. Your secretary suspected, dishonored, and the documents which would have ruined me will soon be destroyed. Heavens, I almost pity you!

(*Vachard returns with Roger.*)

VACHARD: (*pushing Roger*) Here he is.

(*Vachard leaves.*)

FANTÔMAS: I've found what I was looking for. You've kept your word by not betraying me. And I will keep mine. Your fiancée will be released.

ROGER: Ah!

FANTÔMAS: Here are my conditions: my men will escort you to Southampton and you'll embark for America. It's only on the boat that you will meet Miss Emily again. I will provide both of you with the necessary money and false papers. The world will think you guilty and dead. In that way, the police will no longer trouble me. Do you accept my conditions?

ROGER: You are proposing to dishonor me.

FANTÔMAS: You have no other choice. Miss Emily will become your wife in America, or she will die tonight. What is your decision?

ROGER: The choice is so unexpected...

FANTÔMAS: I haven't any time to waste. Do as I say, or oppose me, but make a decision.

ROGER: Death is less terrible than dishonor…

FANTÔMAS: For Emily as well?

ROGER: Ah, Emily...

FANTÔMAS: Listen to your heart. Accept my conditions.

ROGER: But…

FANTÔMAS: Will you accept?

ROGER: I accept.

FANTÔMAS: Most of all, the world must believe you dead. If you allow anyone to suspect your continued existence, if you reveal the truth to anyone at all, if you return to try to exonerate yourself, I will learn of it, and I will strike you dead as surely as I struck Sherlock Holmes. I can reach you, even in America. Emily will suffer an atrocious death first. You, next. Is that understood?

ROGER: Yes.

FANTÔMAS: Come on, I'll accompany you so that no one disturbs you.

(*Vachard returns, excitedly.*)

VACHEROT: We've been betrayed!

FANTÔMAS: What?!

VACHARD: Lestrade has gone to seek reinforcements to arrest us. The door to the street is locked and guarded from the outside.

FANTÔMAS: Who did it?

VACHARD: Dickson must have let the cat out of the bag.

FANTÔMAS: He suspected you; so be it! But me?

VACHARD: He seems to know everything.

FANTÔMAS: Yes! That's why he crushed my injured hand. And imbecile that I was, I screamed.

VACHARD: What shall we do?

FANTÔMAS: First, let's burn the documents! (*to Roger*) Your friend betrayed me. I hold you responsible.

ROGER: I had nothing to do with it!

FANTÔMAS: If you had allayed his suspicions, he wouldn't have figured it out. You'll bear the consequences of your stupidity. If we're arrested, you know what fate awaits your Emily.

ROGER: Don't kill her!

FANTÔMAS: Come on. You already know that I keep my word. Tomorrow, you'll see that I always keep it.

ROGER: This is dreadful!

VACHARD: The coppers are coming!

(*During this entire scene, Fantômas and Vachard are busy hastily shredding and burning the documents in the fireplace.*)

FANTÔMAS: They'll be too late. Vachard, place yourself in front of the fireplace to hide the fire.

(*Lestrade, Dickson and two police officers enter.*)

LESTRADE: In the name of the law, I arrest you.

FANTÔMAS: Is this a joke?

LESTRADE: I am arresting you as an accomplice in the murder of Sherlock Holmes.

FANTÔMAS: I am detective Tom Bob and this arrest is absurd.

LESTRADE: Detective Tom Bob is in Paris. I've just received confirmation.

FANTÔMAS: (*aside*) Hoisted on my own petard! (*to Lestrade*) You must have been misinformed. I'm here, in London!

LESTRADE: There's other evidence against you.

FANTÔMAS: Like what?

LESTRADE: Like your insistence on placing this box into the hands of this dubious individual.

FANTÔMAS: He's my assistant.

DICKSON: Come on then; here's the box.

LESTRADE: This box ought to contain evidence against you.

FANTÔMAS: Open it and we'll see.

LESTRADE: I'm still waiting for the locksmith.

DICKSON: No need! (*with a powerful effort, he opens the box*) There. That's done. Empty! We've been duped.

LESTRADE: Empty?

FANTÔMAS: Where is the evidence that you propose to use to arrest me?

LESTRADE: (*to Dickson*) What did you say?

DICKSON: We've been had once again, Inspector. But… (*looking at the fireplace where the last pages are burning; some pages have fallen outside unburned*)

LESTRADE: What?

DICKSON: Nothing.

FANTÔMAS: I suppose that now, you will no longer prevent me from leaving?

(*Dickson goes to grab the papers not consumed.*)

LESTRADE: Your dubious conduct warrants further investigation. I'm still arresting you.

FANTÔMAS: There's only one culprit! (*pointing to Roger*) That man there.

LESTRADE: What proves it?

FANTÔMAS: His silence, first of all.

DICKSON: Roger, say that you are not the culprit

FANTÔMAS: He won't say it. Mr. Walter was preparing to flee and make it look like a suicide. He left a note on the table. (*hands the letter written by Roger*) I'm the one who stopped him.

LESTRADE: (*reading*) "I admit to being the murderer of my employer…"

ROGER: But…

(*Dickson, on the side, examines the papers he has picked up.*)

VACHARD: (*low to Robert*) Shut up and save your fiancée.

LESTRADE: So! You're free to go. Please accept my apologies.

DICKSON: Let him speak. Are you guilty?

ROGER: Yes.

DICKSON: He's lying. It's not true.

LESTRADE: Do you have accomplices?

ROGER: No. Let this man leave, he's innocent.

DICKSON: (*to Fantômas*) Then, why is it that you've got a cut hand like the murderer of Sherlock Holmes?

(*Dickson tears Fantômas' glove off.*)

LESTRADE: What?

DICKSON: (*showing the papers he rescued*) And why would Roger Walter want to burn these papers that pertain only to a Doctor Garrick? A Sâr Hamashkim and God knows how many others…

(*Dickson gives the papers to Lestrade.*)

FANTÔMAS: (*aside*) Holmes' documents!

LESTRADE: (*to the policemen*) Take these three men to the station. We'll question them tomorrow.

ROGER: Tomorrow! Emily is lost!

FANTÔMAS: Ah! No, I won't allow it. Take care, Inspector, you're playing a dangerous game which may cost you your position. I'm detective Tom Bob, of the Council of Five of Scotland Yard, and if you dare arrest me on the accusations of this callow American youth, it will go very badly for you. I insist, do you hear me, I insist you set me free immediately.

LESTRADE: You can tell all that to the magistrate tomorrow.

ROGER: Stop, Inspector, I must speak to you.

DICKSON: Finally!

ROGER: I'm innocent! This morning, I told you the truth. The letter in which I accuse myself was extorted from me. This man is indeed the murderer. His is the hand which I stabbed the night of the murder! He's Fantômas, the wretch we've been searching for, and yet, and yet–he must be set free!

LESTRADE: What are you saying?

ROGER: I'm saying that he must be set free, because he's taken my fiancée hostage.

DICKSON: What?

ROGER: Emily was taken away by Mrs. Gruff, and hidden in one of their hideouts. And at 10 p.m. tonight, if this man doesn't come to release her, she will be put to death horribly.

DICKSON: Why didn't you tell me that before?

ROGER: I couldn't. He forbade me to speak and you saw how these wretches kept watching me.

LESTRADE: They won't dare put their threat into execution.

FANTÔMAS: Come on. I have hundreds of murders on my conscience. One more or less won't change my sentence, and it will be sweet revenge against this band of amateur detectives.

ROGER: You heard him. Let him go.

LESTRADE: What you're asking of me is impossible.

ROGER: You'll save her life.

LESTRADE: What makes you think he'll spare his victim?

ROGER: I have his word.

LESTRADE: The word of Fantômas?

FANTÔMAS: It's as good as yours.

LESTRADE: In any event, I can't do what you want. I'll mobilize several brigades of Scotland Yard, We'll search the usual hideouts, everywhere.

FANTÔMAS: Be my guest. They might find her head.

ROGER: Oh!

DICKSON: (*wanting to hurl himself on him.*) Wretch! Let me...

LESTRADE: (*stopping him*) Enough! Justice must be served. I'm sorry, sir, but my duty comes before anything else. Arrest this man!

FANTÔMAS: Not yet. (*pulling out a gun*) Fantômas will never be taken alive!

(*He shoots himself and collapses into a chair.*)

LESTRADE: (*to a policeman*) A doctor! Quick! Get a doctor!

FANTÔMAS: It hurts. I'm choking.

DICKSON: Let me see the wound!

FANTÔMAS: Don't touch me! I'm dying!

ROGER: Fantômas, do a good deed before dying. Tell us where Emily is.

FANTÔMAS: Never! Vengeance is good. Even after death.

ROGER: You're going to appear before the great judge. Think of that.

FANTÔMAS: The great judge…

ROGER: Speak. Tell me where Emily is.

FANTÔMAS: Okay, I'll tell you. St James Street… Piccadilly… Oh, I'm dying…

ROGER: St James Street? What number? Speak!

FANTÔMAS: The number? I no longer remember…

ROGER: Speak!

FANTÔMAS: Number… Number 13.

ROGER: She's saved!

FANTÔMAS: Let me rest. (*falling back*)

LESRADE: Is he dead?

ROGER: Not yet.

DICKSON: That's a shame.

LESTRADE: Mr. Dickson, and you, Mr. Walter, I beg you to watch this dying man until the arrival of the medical orderlies who will take him to the prison hospital

ROGER: I'd rather go with you.

LESTRADE: I can't permit it. I order you to remain here and watch over this man. Let's go.

ROGER: But…

(*Lestrade leaves with his men.*)

DICKSON: Let them do it.

ROGER: I wanted to embrace Emily. I wanted to rescue her.

DICKSON: They'll embrace her just as well without you.

ROGER: What?

DICKSON: Sorry, I meant they'll rescue her just as well without you being there! As for kissing, you'll get plenty of that later…

ROGER: Hush! Not in front of a dying man.

DICKSON: Him? He's lucky to be off so easy. He deserves the gibbet a thousand times. Well, Fantômas, here you are, knocked out in the end. I'm not a cruel man, but it pleases me nevertheless. Here I am, nurse to a dying Fantômas. It's a tad unusual, and yet, worth the trouble all the same.

FANTÔMAS: ...Something to drink...

DICKSON: He's thirsty!

ROGER: I'll go get some water.

DICKSON: Why?

ROGER: He's still a man!

DICKSON: Heavens! You've got a pudding instead of a
heart!

(*Roger leaves.*)

DICKSON: And it's to that good lad that this swine did
so much ill. Well, I'm thirsty, too now... I'll
have a drink, but not water! A good glass of
whiskey should do the job.

(*Dickson turns away from Fantômas and pours himself a
drink while all the time keeping an eye on the door.
Fantômas seizes the moment to slip under the table near
the door. The table covering hangs to the floor and hides
him from sight completely.*)

DICKSON: I drink to your health, blackguard, whatever's left of it. Would you like me to pour you
some?

(*Dickson turns round and realizes that Fantômas has
disappeared.*)

DICKSON: What?! (*looking around*) Where did he go? (*putting his glass down and shaking the armchair*) That's impossible!

(*Roger returns with a glass of water that he places on the table.*)

ROGER: What's wrong?

DICKSON: Have you seen Fantômas?

ROGER: Where?

DICKSON: Out there.

ROGER: No.

DICKSON: He isn't here.

ROGER: What does this mean?

DICKSON: He's disappeared.

ROGER: Disappeared!

DICKSON: He left through the ceiling or the floor or he evaporated.

ROGER: (*furious*) You let him escape?

(*During this exchange, Fantômas crawls to the door and disappears.*)

DICKSON: I was between the door and the window. He couldn't pass through here. You didn't see him cross through the kitchen?

ROGER: No one passed that way.

DICKSON: Still, he's gone.

ROGER: That's awful! Because it's obvious now that the address he gave was false, and while Inspector Lestrade is walking into a trap at St James Street, Fantômas is going to kill my Emily at his leisure.

DICKSON: Come on! Calm down!

ROGER: How did this happen?

DICKSON: I don't know, but I'll soon find out. He's not a man, he's the Devil incarnate… What about the cellar? I'll go and take a look!

ROGER: Be careful. Suppose he's lying in wait for you.

DICKSON: Don't worry.

(*Dickson leaves.*)

ROGER: (*shouting*) Is he there?

DICKSON: (*off*) Hurrah!

ROGER: Did you find him?

DICKSON: I found something better.

(*Dickson returns, dragging Vachard behind him.*)

DICKSON: Decidedly, my dear James, we are insepara-
　　　　　ble! There was no way out of the cellar, and
　　　　　you're not a magician, like your master.

VACHARD: Dickson, old pal…

DICKSON: A pal who's going to cause you a heap of
　　　　　pain.

VACHARD: Please let me go. I'm… in… innocent…

DICKSON: Stammer away, my friend, stammer away.

(*Dickson takes the glass of water from the table and
turns his back to the audience, then offers the glass to
Vachard.*)

DICKSON: Here! Drink this to control yourself.

VACHARD: Thanks! (*emptying the glass in one gulp*)

DICKSON: Excellent! You swallowed the drug without
　　　　　making a face.

VACHARD: What drug?

DICKSON: You remember my famous Indian poison?
　　　　　Here's the empty bottle that contained it.

VACHARD: (*fearful*) And the contents?

129

DICKSON: The contents? They're in your stomach by now. See, the remainder of the water is turning green already.

VACHARD: (*turning white*) Assassin!

DICKSON: How well that word sits in your mouth!

(*Vachard rushes toward the door.*)

DICKSON: It's useless to run to the nearest pharmacy. Only I have the antidote. But if I don't give it to you very soon, you'll croak like a mangy dog.

VACHARD: What do you want from me?

DICKSON: (*looking at his watch*) You help us save Miss Emily and deliver Fantômas to us, dead or alive, and I will give you the antidote.

VACHARD: If I do it, you will save my life?

DICKSON: If you don't dawdle. Otherwise, I'll drink to the memory of our old blessed friendship.

VACHARD: Quick, then, follow me!

(*He runs out hurriedly.*)

ROGER: Suppose he prefers death to betraying his master?

DICKSON: Him? Come off it! Never! He's one of those
gallows birds that clings to their own skin.

(*They follow him.*)

C U R T A I N

ACT V

The Lair of Fantômas.

The stage is divided in two by a corridor. To the right and left, there are rooms which are simply furnished and communicate by a door. At the back of the room on the right, there is a window through which rooftops are visible in the background. There is also a desk, chairs, etc. There are doors right and left. There is also a fireplace with a clock above it.

Mrs. Gruff is already there when Fantômas enters.

FANTÔMAS: Mrs. Gruff?

MRS. GRUFF: Ah, there you are at last, Master!

FANTÔMAS: Have you noticed anything unusual about the house?

MRS. GRUFF: Nothing.

FANTÔMAS: The mastiffs have been released in the garden?

MRS. GRUFF: As always.

FANTÔMAS: Very good... And yet, despite all that, I'm experiencing some uneasiness...

MRS. GRUFF: You, Master?

FANTÔMAS: My enemies are tracking me too closely. The struggle is unequal. All against one! Still, I've sworn to conquer, and I will do so.

MRS. GRUFF: You're invincible, Master. A new John Devil.

FANTÔMAS: Let's be less presumptuous. I've just felt the touch of the scaffold.

MRS. GRUFF: My God!

FANTÔMAS: I was almost lost. But all the same, I managed to escape. When it comes to Fantômas, my enemies still have to learn that "almost" is never enough.

MRS. GRUFF: Has all danger disappeared?

FANTÔMAS: I hope so. This hideout is known only to you, Vachard and me. It wasn't even marked in Holmes' papers. I can breathe easier. What about the hostage?

MRS. GRUFF: She's in the padded room. As the hour fixed for your return had passed, I was going to execute your orders just as you came in.

FANTÔMAS: It didn't hurt anything to wait. Bring her to me.

(*Mrs. Gruff goes out.*)

FANTÔMAS: (*alone, lighting a cigarette*) What about

that imbecile of Vachard? Did he get out in time? Bah! Whatever happens, he won't date betray me...

(*Mrs. Gruff returns with Emily in tow.*)

EMILY: Finally, I'm going to learn the truth... (*seeing Fantômas*) Was it you, sir, who lured me into this odious trap?

FANTÔMAS: Indeed it was, Miss.

FANTÔMAS: Then you're the one who murdered my uncle, framed Roger... You're...

FANTÔMAS: Yes, I am Fantômas.

EMILY: Oh! Yet, you seem such a gentleman.

FANTÔMAS: And I am, whenever circumstances permit.

EMILY: You will be one with me, then?

FANTÔMAS: To my great regret, I cannot.

EMILY: What are you saying? No... You seek to frighten me. I know quite well you intend to free me. Mrs. Gruff promised me. She assured me I would be free, if you returned safe and sound.

FANTÔMAS: Yes, if your Roger didn't betray me. But he has, in fact, done so.

EMILY: Ah. (*a pause*) In that case…?

FANTÔMAS: In that case, I have condemned you to death.

EMILY: To death? No, no, sir. Don't do that! You don't have to kill me... I'm young, I'm in love, I have a whole life of happiness ahead of me. I don't want to die! (*falling to her knees*) Please, sir, I am at your feet, spare me! Why would you kill a poor girl who has never harmed anyone? I won't betray you, sir, I swear. Besides, how could I? I don't know where this house is located. You had me brought here blindfolded. Take me out the same way. Take all imaginable precautions, but please, don't kill me. (*bursting into tears*) Please!

FANTÔMAS: Believe me, I regret it very much, Miss Emily. I would have been greatly pleased to show my generosity and set you free.

EMILY: Why can't you still do that?

FANTÔMAS: Because in the situation I'm in, I can only escape by terror. It is absolutely necessary that the very idea of unmasking me makes the rash person who attempts it tremble in fear. I'm done for if it can be said that Fantômas allowed himself to give way because of a woman's tears.

EMILY: Then nothing can save me?

FANTÔMAS: Nothing. I promised the police they would find your head. I must keep my word. (*cocking his revolver*)

EMILY: My head? What do you mean? (*realizing*) Oh My God! Monster! Help! Help!

FANTÔMAS: My poor child, you're making yourself hoarse in vain.

EMILY: (aside) It's obvious he's letting me scream because no help will come. This is horrible! I feel myself becoming mad with terror. If I could go mad, at least, I would no longer know what fate is in store for me. (*To Fantômas*) Please, sir, have mercy!

(*Vachard enters hurriedly.*)

FANTÔMAS: Ah! There you are, Vachard. So much the better. Make this woman be quiet. Her screams are getting on my nerves.

VACHARD: What are you going to do with her?

FANTÔMAS: Kill her.

VACHARD: One moment! What time is it?

FANTÔMAS: (*looking at the clock*) 9:40 p.m. You seem upset. What's wrong with you? Is danger threatening us?

VACHARD: Yes! I must speak to you alone.

FANTÔMAS: So be it! But let's put the girl down first. We will talk afterward. (*raising his revolver*)

VACHARD: (*getting in front of her*) No, let's talk before you execute her.

EMILY: Thank you, sir.

FANTÔMAS: (*puzzled*) Why?

VACHARD: Because… Because we must.

FANTÔMAS: I don't like these caprices. I'm warning you, Vachard, you will give me a plausible explanation for your conduct or join the girl. (*to Mrs. Gruff*) Lock her in the padded room for me.

EMILY: (*to Vachard*) Sir, please speak for me, I beg you.

FANTÔMAS: Go.

(*Mrs. Gruff drags Emily out; they leave.*)

FANTÔMAS: Well, I'm listening to you. What's wrong? Are the police on your trail?

(*Vachard makes a negative sign.*)

FANTÔMAS: So much the better. But then, why this

incomprehensible intervention? Explain yourself. I'm trying in vain to understand. You're not in love with the girl, are you?

(*Vachard shrugs his shoulders.*)

FANTÔMAS: You're my best lieutenant, and yet, right now, I almost don't recognize you anymore. Your eyes have changed… Your face, too... What's wrong with you? (*exploding*) Say something, will you!

(*Outside, the dogs can be heard howling.*)

FANTÔMAS: The dogs are howling. They only howl when death is near. Vachard, why are the dogs howling?

(*Mrs. Gruff reappears in the doorway.*)

MRS. GRUFF: Because they've been poisoned. Our three mastiffs are dying.

FANTÔMAS: I see… Vachard, you've betrayed me.

VACHARD: (*aside*) Only fifteen minutes left, and I don't have a gun!

MRS. GRUFF: Whoever they are, they've sabotaged the bolts. There's no way to close the door.

FANTÔMAS: I'm lost if treason poisons my plans and even my best lieutenants betray me.

MRS. GRUFF: I didn't betray you, Master.

FANTÔMAS: Watch over the girl. At least, don't let that vengeance escape me.

(*Mrs. Gruff exits.*)

FANTÔMAS: The police are down below?

VACHARD: No.

FANTÔMAS: Come on! They have the house surrounded?

VACHARD: No.

RIVERE: Still, you've betrayed me! I see it. I feel it. What price did they offer you for my skin? A fine sum, probably. I hope you didn't sell me out at a discount.

VACHARD: I didn't sell you out.

FANTÔMAS: All the same! You're trembling and lying like a coward.

VACHEROT: I didn't sell you out.

FANTÔMAS: How many are there to get me? Ten? Twenty?

VACHARD: I am all alone.

FANTÔMAS: That's not true. Since you poisoned the

dogs, it must be in order to allow others to enter. Why did you do that? You, in whom I'd placed all my confidence. I had plans for you! To sell me for money!

VACHARD: I didn't sell you out!

FANTÔMAS: Vachard, this comedy has lasted long enough! I'm astonished not to have beaten you like a dog! I'm astonished to see you still alive before me. I must have affection for you that I've never felt for anyone else. But everything comes to an end. Minutes count.

VACHARD: More than you think.

FANTÔMAS: Speak the truth, at last! Do I have an enemy before me, or a madman?

VACHARD: Neither the one nor the other.

FANTÔMAS: Do you want money? How much?

VACHARD: Not a penny!

FANTÔMAS: What then?

VACHARD: Nothing.

(*He tries to seize the revolver, but Fantômas, wise to him, tosses it out the window.*)

FANTÔMAS: Foiled!

VACHARD: So much the worse!

FANTÔMAS: You sought to kill me!

VACHARD: It's necessary. One of us must die. I must kill you and I will.

FANTÔMAS: Vachard!

VACHARD: I love you, Master, but I love myself more! So much the worse for you, because I have no choice. Come on, get ready to die, Fantômas, for I'm going to kill you.

FANTÔMAS: The truth at last! But why do you wish to kill me?

VACHARD: Because Dickson's poisoned me, and the price of the antidote is your death.

FANTÔMAS: The wretch! Ah! This is well played! Look, Vachard, don't go crazy. Let's reason this out...

VACHARD: I have no more time to talk, Master. The poison's making my blood boil. My head's ready to explode.

FANTÔMAS: Still, what if…

VACHARD: No more talk! I have only ten minutes to be saved and all the talk in the world will achieve nothing.
(*Vachard pulls out a knife.*)

VACHARD: Still, I don't want to take you treacherously. I'll make you an honest proposition. Let's fight with our knives. If you die, Dickson will save me. If you're the victor... Well, I prefer to die from a knife rather than being poisoned like a dog.

FANTÔMAS: You're mad!

VACHARD: En garde! Or I'll strike you dead here and now!

FANTÔMAS: Vachard! Listen to me!

VACHARD: You're not a coward. And I've seen you fight before! Fight!

FANTÔMAS: Enough! I am your master and I order you to listen to me.

VACHARD: No more!

FANTÔMAS: Is Dickson here with his antidote?

VACHARD: He's in the street below, awaiting my signal to come up.

FANTÔMAS: To look at a body? How charming. Give the signal.

VACHARD: No! I want an honest battle with you–all or nothing. But I won't risk being betrayed! My life depends on it.

FANTÔMAS: What guarantees do you have that they will give you the antidote once I'm dead?

VACHARD: I have Dickson's word.

FANTÔMAS: Pfft! I've seen Dickson's type before in America. For him, promises made to people like us don't count. Vachard, fear has made you lose your head. I pardon you. By Jove, one has only one skin, after all, and one clings to it! But get hold of yourself and let's act together. Give the signal!

VACHARD: But what if it doesn't work. What if I die poisoned?

FANTÔMAS: Give the signal!

(*Vachard heads towards the window.*)

VACHARD: (*aside*) Oh, the power of this man! How he dominates me even now.

(*He gives a signal.*)

FANTÔMAS: Who's down there?

VACHARD: Harry Dickson and Roger Walter.

FANTÔMAS: Are they both coming?

VACHARD: Yes. I feel a cold sweat all over me.

FANTÔMAS: The fear of death perhaps?

VACHARD: Of dying like this, yes! To have this poison freeze my heart, boil my insides... Quick, Master! Act! Help me! Save me! I have only a few minutes left!

FANTÔMAS: That's plenty.

VACHARD: (*crazy*) The hand of the clock is racing. Why is it going faster than normal?

FANTÔMAS: Vachard! They're coming. Calm down. Or will you ruin us!

VACHARD: Yes, be calm... Give me your orders, Master. I'm listening.

(*Fantômas whispers to him. Meanwhile, Dickson and Roger Walter have entered the corridor.*)

DICKSON: We've already found the dead dogs in the garden outside. May Fantômas be found dead inside as well, and all will be well.

ROGER: A shame about the dogs.

DICKSON: Yes, but it won't be a shame for Fantômas!

FANTÔMAS: (*inside the room*) Mrs. Gruff!

(*Mrs. Gruff enters.*)

FANTÔMAS: Go set the trap for our visitors.

(*Mrs. Gruff leaves.*)

DICKSON: Stay here, Roger.

ROGER: No! We'll go in together.

DICKSON: But if it's a trap, who will come save us if we're both in its snare?

ROGER: I sent a note to Inspector Lestrade.

DICKSON: Oh! In that case, we'll have plenty of time to die, be buried, and resurrected!

ROGER: So be it! I'll stay!

(*In the meantime, Vachard has tied up Fantômas as per the villain's instructions. Dickson opens the door and enters.*)

DICKSON: Here I am.

VACHARD: As you can see, I've kept my word. There's Fantômas all tied up.

DICKSON: Very well. And Miss Emily?

VACHARD: Over this way, safe and sound!

DICKSON: Free her.

(*Vachard opens the door and Emily enters.*)

VACHARD: Come out, Miss Emily, you're free.

EMILY: Saved by your intervention. Oh! Thank you!

DICKSON: You've kept your word, I'll keep mine.

(*He pulls a small vial from his pocket.*)

EMILY: You here, Mr. Dickson? What joy!

DICKSON: It's great pleasure to see you, Miss Emily, but I know someone who will be even more pleased.

EMILY: Roger.

DICKSON: Go look over there.

(*Emily goes out into the corridor and falls into Roger's arms.*)

EMILY: Roger!

ROGER: Emily!

(*They embrace.*)

VACHARD: (*to Dickson*) I've done all you've asked of me. Quick, the antidote!

DICKSON: Here it is. (*handing him the vial*)

VACHARD: Ah! Just in time!

(*He tries to remove the cork from the vial. Roger and Emily take their leave silently.*)

DICKSON: (*suddenly looking at Fantômas*) Why, those bonds won't hold.

(*He rushes toward Fantômas. From behind, Vachard strikes him with a cudgel, delivering a blow to the head. Dickson falls over.*)

VACHARD: Take that!

DICKSON: (*falling*) Oh! I'm knocked out!

(*Fantômas frees himself from the ropes.*)

ROGER: That shout! They're killing Harry!

(*He rushes back, enters the room, sees Dickson on the ground and smacks Vachard on the arm just as the bandit was about to take the antidote.*)

ROGER: Wretch! You won't escape!

(*The vial of antidote falls to the ground near Roger's feet; Roger stomps on it.*)

VACHARD: No! Not the antidote! I'm lost!

(*The cloak strikes ten. Roger kneels by Harry Dickson. Fantômas gets ready to flee, but Vachard stops him.*)

VACHARD: (*seizing Fantômas by the throat*) Ah, no! You won't get out of this alive while I die here like a dog because of you! You're responsible for my death. You will pay for it.

(*Fantômas and Vachard struggle by the window.*)

FANTÔMAS: Let me go, you fool!

VACHARD: We'll take the great leap together.

DICKSON: (*getting up*) Very interesting match. I'll keep score.

VACHARD: Help!

(*Fantômas, with a superhuman effort, lifts Vachard and pushes him through the window. However, Vachard manages to cling desperately to Fantômas. The two fall into the void.*)

DICKSON: Bon voyage! What an idea those two wretches had to leave through the window.

EMILY: Here's Inspector Lestrade!

DICKSON: So soon! He's turning into the Cavalry!

(*Lestrade enters, followed by Mrs. Gruff, held between two policemen.*)

DICKSON: And there's dear Mrs. Gruff! What a happy family!

ROGER: (*to Dickson*) Thank you, Harry! You're the one who saved us!

DICKSON: Maybe I'll inherit the mantle of Sherlock Holmes? By Jove! I could become the new King of Detectives!

CURTAIN

EPILOG
(by Frank J. Morlock)

A small cemetery in London. A freshly dug grave with a modest tombstone. The stage is empty. Roger Walter, Emily and Harry Dickson enter. Roger and Emily have been quarreling.

ROGER: But I haven´t done anything wrong!

EMILY: It´s what you're going to do.

DICKSON: Miss Emily, be reasonable...

EMILY: No! I won´t marry Roger if he persists in his plan!

ROGER: (*upset, turns away*) It's impossible to reason with you.

EMILY: (*changing the subject*) My poor uncle... (*pointing to a tomb*)

DICKSON: He´ll be missed.

(*An old man with a cane walks feebly towards them, coming from the same direction as they. Inspector Lestrade enters from the opposite direction.*)

LESTRADE: Ah, there you are!

(*Lestrade exchanges bows with Roger and Emily, mak-*

ing consoling gestures, and casts a dark eye towards Dickson.)

LESTRADE: Well, I confess we never really got along, but he was the greatest of detectives. (*takes off his hat*)

(*After a moment's silence, they prepare to leave.*)

ROGER: (*returning to his concern*) After a decent interval, Miss Emily, I hope that you'll agree to marry me as we planned.

EMILY: You'll give up your ridiculous idea of becoming a detective?

ROGER: (*pause*) But what shall I do instead?

EMILY: Papa needs a manager for the estate. He's getting on in years, you know…

ROGER: (*pensive*) Working for Mr. Sherrinford…

DICKSON: (*suddenly*) You know, I've been thinking of becoming a detective myself.

EMILY: You, Mr. Dickson?

DICKSON: I'm not joking. I think I have a real flair for it.

ROGER: We made a good team, didn't we, Harry? We didn't do too bad of a job, did we? We could become partners

EMILY: (*furious, to Roger*) In that case, you can marry someone else!

ROGER: Emily!

LESTRADE: (*trying to be helpful*) I think they really did a good job, Miss Emily.

EMILY: (*turning on him*) Mind your own business, Inspector! (*to Roger*) I refuse to be worried every time you leave the house.

ROGER: But I'm smart.

DICKSON: And I'm even smarter.

EMILY: Not as smart as my uncle.

DICKSON: Of course, we wouldn't compare ourselves to the Master.

(*The strange old man has come close to them.*)

EMILY I should hope not!

DICKSON: But I'm at least as smart as Lestrade here.

LESTRADE: Humph!

DICKSON: Oh, I mean that as a compliment, Inspector.

LESTRADE: Apology accepted.

DICKSON: So you see there's nothing to worry about.

EMILY: My uncle was smarter than the two of you put together…

(*The old man chuckles.*)

EMILY: …But see what happened to him… (*pointing to the gravestone*) And it might easily happen to you. Or to you too, Mr. Dickson. No, I won't marry you, Roger. (*she begins sobbing*)

LESTRADE: I'd better be going.

OLD MAN: Stay, if you would, Lestrade.

EMILY: That voice…

LESTRADE: (*looking at the old man*) Holmes!

ROGER: (*astonished*) Master?

DICKSON: You're not dead?

HOLMES Obviously, since I'm not a ghost. Lestrade, here, knew the truth, since I obviously couldn't hide it from him. Faking my death was the only way of bringing Fantômas out of hiding and getting him not only to reveal his true identity, but those of his whole scurrilous crew…

(*There is a movement in the heavy shrubbery behind the grave, very slight, but noticeable to the audience.*)

EMILY: (*running to Holmes*) Uncle! Uncle Sherlock!

HOLMES: (*slightly embarrassed*) There, there… (*handing her off to Roger, who holds her*) Marry him, Emily.

EMILY But I don´t want him to be killed!

ROGER: (*sighing*) I won't be. I'm through with that. I'll go work for your father.

EMILY: (*beaming*) Excellent. And what about Mr. Dickson?

HOLMES: He won't die, any more than I did. Great detectives never die, and I predict that he will be a great detective.

DICKSON: (*proud*) Thank you, sir. I'll do my best to make you proud!

EMILY: (*unconvinced*) Are you sure? (*thoughtfully*) But how did you escape that fiend Fantômas?

HOLMES: I was expecting an attack, after I realized that our new housekeeper, Mrs. Gruff, was a spy. I put a dummy in my place every night.

EMILY: Even so, I'm still worried...

LESTRADE: Don't be. Listen to Mr. Holmes, Miss. I've learned that Sherlock Holmes is always right, Even when I'm convinced he's wrong. And in this case, for once, I find myself in total agreement with him. As much as it pains me to admit it, I think Mr. Dickson will make a great detective.

DICKSON: Besides, Fantômas appears to be dead, although the body could not be found. (*puzzled*) But still, why have this funeral and burial?

HOLMES: A detective makes enemies, not friends, Dickson, and this may earn me a few more years of peace… After all, this is not the first time Sherlock Holmes has died and been resurrected. Come now, Emily, give Roger your hand.

(*Slowly, Emily allows Holmes to place her hand in Roger Walter's. Then, she leans against him lovingly, while Harry Dickson looks at them wistfully.*)

(*They move away. As they leave, Fantômas, who had been hiding and listening in the shadows, emerges and shakes his fist at the retreating group.*)

FANTÔMAS: I thought as much. We shall meet again, Mr. Holmes. And next time, you shall not be so lucky, nor I so stupid.

FINAL CURTAIN

Afterword

What changes were introduced in our adaptation of *Bandits in Black Coats*, and how are they reconciled with the official chronologies of the various characters featured in it?

Sherlock Holmes:

The play was originally entitled *The Murder of Herlock Sholmes*, using the transparent alias devised by Maurice Leblanc to disguise the name of the Great Detective. In 1907, the only canonical text was *The Adventure of the Lion's Mane* in which a retired Holmes investigates the death of Professor McPherson and confesses an unusual attraction for the beautiful Maud Bellamy. There is no great conflict in imagining Holmes returning to London the year before to set an elaborate trap for Fantômas. His "resurrection" in the epilog written by Frank Morlock is, of course, an addition to the original play. Holmes crosses swords with Fantômas again in Frank J. Morlock's original play, *The Grand Horizontals*,[8] which takes place in the spring of 1907, and in which the master villain explicitly talks about "renewing their acquaintance."

Holmes' niece, bearing the rather un-English name of "Bertha" in the original play, was rechristened "Emily" in this edition. She is the daughter of Holmes' older brother, Sherrinford.

---

[8] Available in a Black Coat Press edition (ISBN 9781932983470).

Fantômas:

At the end of Pierre Souvestre & Marcel Allain's sixth novel, *Le Policier Apache*, Fantômas leaves Paris in the summer of 1905 to find refuge in London, where he hides under the identities of detective Tom Bob and Docteur Garrick. He resurfaces only in April 1908 in the seventh episode, *Le Pendu de Londres*, and from there, travels to South Africa for the events of *The Daughter of Fantômas*.[9] We know very little of his activities during 1906 and 1907, other than his liaison with Françoise Lemercier, his rise in the secret hierarchy of Scotland Yard and his blackmailing of Lord Ascott.

In the play, the character of the mysterious, elusive, phantasmic arch-villain is named "Doctor Rivier." Only Holmes believes in his existence. The *Fantômas* series had just run its course a year before the play and, like Sir Arthur Conan Doyle's stories, had already spawned a whole gallery of Fantômas imitators. It is our contention that "Dr. Rivier" and Fantômas are one and the same, just as "Herlock Sholmes" is really Sherlock Homes.

Harry Dickson:

In the play, the young hero is named "J. J. Davidson" and is a little older than Harry Dickson, who, in 1907, would be 18 and a student at the University of South Kensington in London. However, like Dickson, "Davidson" is American, skilled at boxing, and wants to become a detective.

To the extent that Harry Dickson (who started his literary existence as an avatar of Sherlock Holmes) was later depicted as a "student" of Holmes, a role confirmed

---

[9] Available in a Black Coat Press edition (ISBN 9781932983562).

by his appearance (as Allan Dickson) in the 1912 Arthur Galopin novel *L'Homme au Complet Gris*, there was no reason to not turn young "J.J. Davidson" into Harry Dickson.

Dickson's past is littered with long-lost and unrequited loves and women "who got away." Emily Holmes is one more name added to a list that includes Irène de Hautefeuille and Georgette Cuvelier.

The Black Coats:

Paul Féval's criminal empire, called the *Habits Noirs* in French, is referenced in the original title *Bandits en habit noir*, which, as we noted in the introduction, was also one of the titles used in the 1908 *Nick Carter* serial. The notion that Fantômas was loosely connected to that sinister criminal brotherhood was initiated by Alfredo Castelli in his story "Long Live Fantômas!" published in *Tales of the Shadowmen, Volume 3*. The Black Coats do not actively figure in the play, but their evil shadow still looms over the story through their catch phrases *to pay the law*, *cut the branch*, etc. used here by Fantômas.

Jean-Marc Lofficier

A CHRONOLOGY OF TERROR
by Jean-Marc Lofficier
(incorporating research from Etienne Barillier)

1867. Fantômas and Juve were born in Brittany. They were brothers. Their mother's first name was Anne-Marie; her last name is unknown, and so is their father.

I have speculated that Fantômas was the son of Rocambole and his foe/lover Ellen Palmure, while Juve was the son of Ellen and Armand de Kergaz, a Breton nobleman who was also Rocambole's foe and occasional ally. One might speculate that "Anne-Marie" was either an alias of Ellen Palmure, or the name of the nurse who raised the children.

Rocambole met Ellen in Les Misères de Londres *which takes place in 1867-68, so the dates fit. The Breton connection assumes that Ellen chose to give birth in Brittany under said alias to avoid the stigma of being an unwed mother.*

1868. The children were separated soon after birth. According to the canon, Juve was raised in a public orphanage. We do not know who raised Fantômas.

Based on Arnould Galopin's L'Homme au Complet Gris (The Man in Grey)*, a novel in which Sherlock Holmes and Harry Dickson again meet Fantômas, I have speculated that Fantômas was raised in the village of Lyndhurst in Sussex by Ellen Palmure's old henchman, Reverend Paterson. This theory will be more fully developed in our translation/adaptation of Galopin's novel. According to it, the young man who would grow* *up to become Fantômas met Lord Edward Beltham for the first time as a boy.*

1885. The future Fantômas traveled to India.

Rocambole had been in India 20 years before. It is possible that young Fantômas went there to collect some kind of inheritance.

While in India, Fantômas exerted an evil influence over Sandyck, the son of Bedjapur, an Indian king, and caused him to betray his father to the British.

1886. Sandyck had a daughter with an otherwise unidentified European woman. That daughter was Hélène.

In La Fin de Fantômas, *Souvestre and Allain claimed that Helen was Sandyck's daughter. But maybe she really was Fantômas' biological daughter. Juve claimed to have found documents that incontrovertibly proved that Hélène was not Fantômas' biological daughter, but there could be lies within lies – Juve lying, the documents lying... Certainly, Fantômas always behaved as if Hélène really was his daughter...*

1887. Sandyck was killed by Bedjapur's followers. To protect baby Hélène from their further wrath, she was taken to South Africa where she was raised by Laetitia. Bedjapur eventually moved to Paris.

1888. The affair of Dr. Moreau and the Jack the Ripper murders in London. Lord Edward Beltham was connected to both cases and was forced to leave England soon thereafter.

This is a combination of facts presented in both L'Homme au Complet Gris *and Alfredo Castelli's short story "Long Live Fantômas!"*

1890-92. The future Fantômas, by then calling himself Archduke Juan North, operated in the German Principality of Heisse-Weimar. There, he married a woman whose identity was unrevealed, but who was the aunt of the future king, Fredrick-Christian. They had a son: Vladimir.

In circumstances as yet unrevealed–Souvestre and Allain only mention a "big scandal"–North was arrested and sent to prison.

During that time, Juve grew up, joined the French police and embarked on a career at the Sûreté.

Fantômas once told Juve that he was a former ball and chain convict; presumably, this is when his incarceration took place. We don't know where Fantômas was incarcerated, not how and when he escaped.

1893. A criminal known as Fantômas terrorized Berlin.

According to Alfredo Castelli, the mention by Marcel Allain of a criminal known as Fantômas in Berlin in 1893 in The Fantômas of Berlin *proves that there was another Fantômas operating in Europe before Gurn. In "Long Live Fantômas!" Castelli theorizes that this earlier Fantômas was none other than the depraved Lord Edward Beltham, a dangerous serial killer.*

1895. French industrialist Charles Rambert and his wife, Alice, had a son: Etienne, who later became Jerôme Fandor.

1896. The future Fantômas, known as the "Pallid Mask," became involved in a murderous conspiracy and power play amongst the Black Coats. (*Rick Lai's "Corridors of Deceit"*)

1897. The future Fantômas and Charles Rambert were business partners and friends in New York. Alice and baby Charles remained in France. According to Souvestre and Allain, Etienne Rambert was one of the very few people who knew his partner' real name.

Could Fantômas really have had an affair with Alice Rambert and be Fandor's biological father, as some have supposed? All things considered, it is unlikely. Charles appears to have been born before Fantômas met Etienne. But nothing completely rules it out either...

One might suppose that it was at that time that Fantômas adopted the alias of Gurn.

1898. Gurn ruined Etienne Rambert. He then traveled to Mexico. There, he took control of a local gang and created a lair to keep his treasure. Afterwards, he embarked for South Africa. There, he joined the Boers and started a diamond smuggling ring with Hans Elders.

Gurn later claimed that he had a baby daughter with an unidentified Boer woman from Pretoria. Was this true? There is no way to know for certain.

1899. The Boer War started (October). Gurn betrayed the Boers, joined the British Army, became an artillery sergeant under the command of Lord Roberts, and used the war to loot and pillage. Gurn renewed his acquaintance with Lord Beltham, and met his much younger wife, Maud, whom he immediately desired.

According to Castelli's "Long Live Fantômas!", during that time, Gurn became Lord Beltham's willing accomplice and partner, some would say spiritual heir, in his sadistic and murderous activities. Lord Beltham's crimes as Fantômas were known to the criminal bro-

therhood called the Black Coats, who condemedn him to
death and chose Gurn to become his executioner.

1900. (May) Gurn left South Africa to return to England
with the Belthams. His affair with Lady Beltham began
on the ship taking them back to England.
  Souvestre and Allain tell us that Gurn entrusted his
baby daughter to Laetitia. But when he returned to South
Africa in The Daughter of Fantômas, *Hélène was too old*
to have been that baby. One possible explanation is that
Gurn lied. He never had a baby girl in Pretoria at all.
Hélène is indeed his biological daughter, the product of
his earlier affair in India with the mysterious European
woman who was Sandyck's wife. Gurn was the one who
entrusted Hélène to Laetitia.
  The documents inside the skull might have estab-
lished Hélène's claim to some kind of Indian title and
fortune. If Juve read them, that woukd be the reason he
believed that Gurn was not Hélène's father. But Gurn
knew that Hélène was really his daughter, and not San-
dyck's, which was why he cared deeply for her. At the
same time, if that truth became known, Hélène stood to
lose a fortune. This is why, throughout the series,
Fantômas murdered everyone who learned the truth of
Hélène's birth.
  During the summer, Lord Beltham surprised Gurn
and his wife together in bed in his apartment Rue Lavert
in Paris. Gurn then strangled him and assumed the mantle of Fantômas. Also that summer, Gurn, posing as
Etienne Rambert, had Alice committed to an asylum.
Towards the end of that year, the new Fantômas killed
the Marquise de Langrune and framed his "son," young
Charles Rambert. (*Fantômas*)

1901. (June) Princess Sonia Danidoff was assaulted by Fantômas in a Parisian Hotel. During the summer, Juve discovered that the real Etienne Rambert died on the *Lancaster*, which was blown up in August by Fantômas, in order to enable him to continue to impersonate his former associate. At Juves's behest, young Charles Rambert became Jerôme Fandor. In August, Gurn was arrested and, at the end of that year, condemned to death. (*Fantômas*)

1902. (January) Fantômas escaped the guillotine by substituting an actor named Valgrand in his place. (*Fantômas*)

(February) Fantômas, using the identity of Dr. Chaleck, escaped from Juve's clutches by blowing up the Belthams' residence. (*Juve contre Fantômas*)

(Spring) "The Tarot of Fantômas."

(June) Lady Beltham and Fantômas attended the coronation of King Edward VII in England, then traveled to America.

Gurn had already spent time in America in 1897. Throughout his career, Fantômas considered the U.S. as one of his safe havens. He also relied on the help of a powerful network of American criminals to blow up a ship like the Lancaster *and create a deep cover such as that of Tom Bob.*

1904. (April) Fantômas, back in France under the disguise of the banker Nanteuil, murdered the painter Jacques Dollon, in order to steal his identity. (*Le Mort qui tue*)

(May) Fantômas, using the twin aliases of the tramp Vagualame and the Baron Naarboveck, became involved in an espionage case. (*L'Agent Secret*)

166

(Summer) Lady Beltham found refuge in Heisse-Weimar as Archduchess Alexandra.

(December) Fantômas kidnapped King Frederick-Christian II of Heisse-Weimar. (*Un Roi Prisonnier de Fantômas*)

1905. (January) Fandor freed the King. At the Gare du Nord, Lady Beltham surrendered the Red Diamond to the King. Mistaken for Fantômas, Juve was arrested. (*Un Roi Prisonnier de Fantômas*)

(May) Fantômas impersonated American detective Tom Bob and investigated his own case.

(July) Juve was freed. Fantômas escaped to England. (*Le Policier Apache*)

1906. While in London, Fantômas operated under the various aliases of Tom Bob (under which he gained membership in the Council of Five of Scotland Yard), Dr. Garrick and Sâr Hamashkim.

First clash between Sherlock Holmes, assisted by a young Harry Dickson, and Fantômas. (*Sherlock Holmes vs. Fantômas*)

1907. (April) Second encounter between Sherlock Holmes and Fantômas. (*The Grand Horizontals*)

Fantômas had an affair with Françoise Lemercier, and plotted to blackmail Lord Ascott. (*Le Pendu de Londres*)

1908. (April) Fantômas kidnapped Fandor and shipped him to South Africa in a crate. He also sent Françoise to America to escape the wrath of a jealous Lady Beltham. (*Le Pendu de Londres*)

(May) Fantômas was arrested by Scotland Yard. In South Africa, Fandor was interned in an asylum, but escaped. (*Le Pendu de Londres* and *La Fille de Fantômas*)

(June) Fantômas was condemned to hang. With Juve's help, he faked death and escaped. (*Le Pendu de Londres* and *La Fille de Fantômas*)

(July) Fantômas travelled to South Africa, unleashing the plague aboard the *British Queen*. Juve followed. Fandor met Hélène and fell in love with her. (*La Fille de Fantômas*)

(December) Back in Paris, Fantômas renewed his affair with Lady Beltham and sought Hélène, who was hiding in the disguise of a department store clerk. Hélène became an outlaw, and escaped. (*Le Fiacre de Nuit*)

1909. (January) Fantômas challenged Irma Vep of the Vampires gang. ("A Dance of Night and Death")

(February) Fantômas took over the *Skobeleff*, a Russian destroyer, and looted the casino of Monte-Carlo. (*La Main Coupée*)

(March) Fantômas wrecked the *Skobeleff* on the Brittany coast. Hélène was arrested, but escaped again. (*L'Arrestation de Fantômas*)

(April) Fantômas was arrested–in Belgium. (*L'Arrestation de Fantômas*)

(November) Juve helped Fantômas escape from his Belgian prison in order to arrest him in France. Fantômas took on the disguise of Investigating Magistrate Charles Pradier. (*Le Magistrat Cambrioleur*)

(December) Fantômas robbed the American millionaire Blackfelder and clashed with Hélène, then known as the Wasp. (*La Livrée du Crime*)

1910. (January) Fantômas returned to America to arrange the theft of gold bullion that was going to be transported across the Atlantic on the SS *Triumph*.

While in New York, Fantômas, using the identity of Melvil, tangled with Nick Carter. (*Nick Carter vs. Fantômas*)

(February) Juve and Fandor thwarted the *Triumph* robbery. Juve was believed to have died in the fire at his apartment Rue Bonaparte. (*La Mort de Juve*)

(March) Fantômas impersonated Juve, but was thwarted when the policeman returned (*L'Evadée de Saint-Lazare*)

(April) Juve and Fandor dismantled Fantômas' smuggling ring on the Spanish border in Western France. Fandor went to Spain to look for Hélène who was kidnapped by a Spanish prince (*La Disparition de Fandor*)

(July) Fandor freed Hélène. Fantômas tried to marry a Spanish princess but was almost captured. His fiancée died. (*Le Mariage de Fantômas*)

(August) Lady Beltham appeared to have been killed by a criminal impersonating Fantômas. It turned out to be Dick Valgrand, the son of the actor guillotined in lieu of Fantômas. (*L'Assassin de Lady Beltham*)

(August) Juve sought the identity of Lady Beltham's murderer. (*La Guêpe Rouge*)

(September) Lady Beltham returned from the dead. She killed Dick Valgrand and his lover, Sarah Gordon. Then, horrified by her crime, committed suicide (September 21). (*La Guêpe Rouge*)

(Late September) Fantômas became involved in an insurance scam. (*Les Souliers du Mort*)

(October) Fantômas' son, Vladimir, competed with his father to steal a fortune from Hesse-Weimar.

Fantômas killed Vladimir's wife, Princess Alexandra. Hélène was arrested in Belgium, but escaped. She joined a circus under the alias of Mogador. (*Le Train Perdu*)

(November) Sonia Danidoff had an affair with Fantômas. Fantômas killed Gérard, a man who knew the truth about Hélène's origins. Fantômas made Hélène swear to never marry Fandor. (*Le Train Perdu*)

1911. (February) The rivalry between Fantômas and Vladimir continued. Vladimir fell in love with Firmaine, then revolted against his father and tried to kill him, but succeeded only in blinding him (temporarily). (*Les Amours d'un Prince*)

(Spring) Fantômas, using the alias of Jap, rebuilt his criminal network in Paris.

(Summer) Fantômas traveled to England to settle an old case regarding his participation in Lord Beltham's crimes. He crossed path with Sherlock Holmes and Harry Dickson again (*L'Homme au Complet Gris*)

(October) Fantômas and Vladimir renewed their battle. Fantômas killed Firmaine. Vladimir threatened Helene's life. Fantômas blew up the Montmartre reservoir. (*Le Bouquet Tragique*)

Fantômas and Vladimir reconciled. Vladimir was arrested after Juve thwarted a horse racing scam. (*Le Jockey Masqué*)

(November) Vladimir was on trial. Fantômas succeeded in arranging his release. (*Le Cercueil Vide*)

(December) Fantômas tried to put Hélène on the throne of Holland. Fandor discovered that his father Etienne had not died after all, but Etienne expired just as he was about to tell his son Fantômas' real name. (*Le Faiseur de Reines*)

(Late December) Fantômas impersonated Etienne Rambert one last time as Fandor met his mother again. Fantômas kidnapped Hélène and sent her to Mexico. (*Le Cadavre Géant*)

1912. (January-March) In Mexico, Helen fought Vladimir for the secret of Fantômas' treasure, which was kept in a hidden lair. Fantômas and Juve arrived in Mexico. Juve killed Vladimir just as he was about to kill Helene. (*Le Voleur d'Or* and *La Série Rouge*)

(April) In Switzerland, Fantômas tried to kill Fandor. Alice Rambert died. Fantômas convinced Hélène that Fandor is unfaithful to her. (*L'Hôtel du Crime*)

(April) In Russia, Fantômas impersonated the head of the Tsar's secret police. Hélène reconciled with Fandor. Fantômas stole a diamond necklace and returned to France. (*La Cravate de Chanvre*)

(April) Fantômas struck in Paris! He killed Bedjapur just as the Indian king was going to reveal the identity of Hélène's mother. (*La Fin de Fantômas*)

(April 10) Juve, Fandor, Hélène and Fantômas embarked on the *Titanic*. (*La Fin de Fantômas*)

(April 15) The *Titanic* sank. Fandor and Hélène escaped. Fantômas and Juve are believed to have died. (*La Fin de Fantômas*)

According to comments made by Allain, the ship was indeed supposed to be Titanic, *but the name was changed to that of* Gigantic, *in order to not offend the memories of the victims. (*La Fin de Fantômas *was published on September 20, 1913, less than 18 months after the tragic events.) The authors' intention, at the time, was to have the two protagonists, Juve and Fantômas, die after the ultimate revelation that they were brothers,* *while Fandor and Hélène went on to live happily ever after. Pierre Souvestre died on February 26, 1914, and the recorded canon of Fantômas stops at that point.*

Due to popular demand, Marcel Allain decided to restart the series in 1925, and produced 11 volumes, the last being serialized (but never collected in book form) in 1963. Allain died on August 25, 1969. Most Fantômas *scholars do not consider these stories canonical, for the most part because the characters (including Lady Beltham, back from the dead without any explanations given) do not age, being just the same in the 1960s as they were in the 1910s.* Fantômas mène le bal, *the final novel written by Allain, has Fantômas and Juve trapped in a rocket and shot into outer space.*

Johan Heliot penned a sequel to that novel, entitled "Vous rêvez trop de Fantômas" (or "Fantômas 1970"), in which both Fantômas and Juve return to Earth as electromagnetic beings, having been transformed by the alien Capellans. Curiously, the Capellans are one of the two warring alien races mentioned by Philip José Farmer in The Other Log of Phileas Fogg.

Other stories featuring the return of Fantômas, ignoring the Allain sequels, are:

1916. "Trauma," in which Fantômas returned to Paris to murder Vladimir, or a man impersonating his dead son.

1912-17. *Fantômas in America*, a novel in which Fantômas returned to America; the main action took place in 1917 New York, on the eve of America entering the Great War. His plot was to capture Professor Harrington, the only man to know the secret of Eldorado and gold-making. His adversary was Detective Frederick Dickson, a cousin of Harry Dickson.

Fantômas in America *is inspired by the long-lost 1920 American* Fantômas *serial written by Edward Sedwick & George Eshenfelder for the Fox Film Corporation, released in France under the title of* Diabolos, *due to Marcel Allain's objections. A mysterious "Woman in Black" might be Lady Beltham, thus reconciling this version with that of Marcel Allain's sequels.*

1921. "A Jest to Pass the Time," in which an older Fantômas duelled with Zenith and competed with various rivals to steal the Moonstone.

Bibliography

Novels by Pierre Souvestre & Marcel Allain (all published by Fayard):

1911:

1. *Fantômas*
2. *Juve contre Fantômas* (*The Exploits of Juve / The Silent Executioner*)
3. *Le Mort qui tue* (*Messengers of Evil*)
4. *L'Agent Secret* (*A Nest of Spies*)
5. *Un Roi Prisonnier de Fantômas* (*A Royal Prisoner*)
6. *Le Policier Apache* (*The Long Arm of Fantômas*)
7. *Le Pendu de Londres* (*Slippery as Sin*)
8. *La Fille de Fantômas* (*The Daughter of Fantômas*) (Black Coat Press, 2006, ISBN 978-1-932983-56-2)
9. *Le Fiacre de Nuit*
10. *La Main Coupée* (*The Limb of Satan*)
11. *L'Arrestation de Fantômas*
12. *Le Magistrat Cambrioleur*

1912:

13. *La Livrée du Crime*
14. *La Mort de Juve*
15. *L'Evadée de Saint-Lazare*
16. *La Disparition de Fandor*
17. *Le Mariage de Fantômas*
18. *L'Assassin de Lady Beltham*
19. *La Guêpe Rouge*
20. *Les Souliers du Mort*
21. *Le Train Perdu*
22. *Les Amours d'un Prince*
23. *Le Bouquet Tragique*

1913:

24. *Le Jockey Masqué*

25. *Le Cercueil Vide*
26. *Le Faiseur de Reines*
27. *Le Cadavre Géant*
28. *Le Voleur d'Or*
29. *La Série Rouge*
30. *L'Hôtel du Crime*
31. *La Cravate de Chanvre*
32. *La Fin de Fantômas*

Novels by Marcel Allain:
Fantômas of Berlin (Brentano's, 1919)
1. *Fantômas est-il ressuscité?* (SPE, 1925) (*The Lord of Terror*)
2. *Fantômas, Roi des Recéleurs* (1926) (*Juve in the Dock*)
3. *Fantômas en Danger* (1926) (*Fantômas Captured*)
4. *Fantômas Prend sa Revanche* (1926) (*The Revenge of Fantômas*)
5. *Fantômas Attaque Fandor* (1926) (*Bulldog and Rats*)
6. *Si c'était Fantômas?* (serial. in *Le Petit Journal*, 1933)
7. *Oui, c'est Fantômas!* (serial. in *Le Petit Journal*, 1934)
8. *Fantômas Joue et Gagne* (serial. in *La Dépêche*, 1935)
9. *Fantômas Rencontre l'Amour* (serial. in *France-Soir*, 1946)
10. *Fantômas Vole des Blondes* (serial. in *Ce Soir*, 1948)
11. *Fantômas Mène le Bal* (serial. in *Constellation*, 1963)

Other Works:

Nick Carter vs. Fantômas by Alexandre Bisson & Guillaume Livet (1910) (Black Coat Press, 2007, ISBN 978-1-934543-05-4)

L'Homme au Complet Gris by Arnould Galopin (1912)

Sherlock Holmes vs. Fantômas by Pierre de Wattyne & Yorril Walter (1914) (Black Coat Press, 2009, ISBN 978-1-934543-67-2)

Sherlock Holmes: The Grand Horizontals by Frank J. Morlock (Black Coat Press, 2006, ISBN 978-1-932983-47-0)

Fantômas in America by David White (Black Coat Press, 2007, ISBN 978-1-934543-07-8)

Short Stories:

"Trauma" by Bill Cunningham in *Tales of the Shadowmen 2: Gentlemen of the Night* (Black Coat Press, 2006, ISBN 978-1-932983-60-9)

"The Tarot of Fantômas" by Jean-Marc Lofficier in *Tales of the Shadowmen 2: Gentlemen of the Night*

"A Jest to Pass the Time" by Jess Nevins in *Tales of the Shadowmen 2: Gentlemen of the Night*

"Vous rêvez trop de Fantômas" by Johan Heliot in *Les Nombreuses Vies de Fantômas* (Les Moutons Electriques, 2006, ISBN 978-2-915793-24-6)

"Long Live Fantômas!" by Alfredo Castelli in *Tales of the Shadowmen 3: Danse Macabre* (Black Coat Press, 2007, ISBN 978-1-932983-77-7)

"A Dance of Night and Death" by Travis Hiltz in *Tales of the Shadowmen 3: Danse Macabre*

"Corridors of Deceit" by Rick Lai in *Tales of the Shadowmen 4: Lords of Terror* (Black Coat Press, 2008, ISBN 978-1-934543-02-3)

BLACK COAT PRESS